# THE LOST GIRLS

## Mary Shelley Investigations
### Book Two

## Donna Gowland

SAPERE
BOOKS

# THE LOST GIRLS

Published by Sapere Books.

24 Trafalgar Road, Ilkley, LS29 8HH

saperebooks.com

ISBN: 978-0-85495-725-5

*To Fred and Darcy.*

*'You are now in London,*
*That great sea,*
*Whose ebb and flow*
*At once is deaf and loud.'*

Percy Shelley, 1824

# ACKNOWLEDGEMENTS

There are too many people to dedicate this book to, so I would like to give a big shout-out to all these wonderful people: Andrea Jaeger, Natalie Woodhead, Lisa Burke, Laura Berry, Eileen Miles, Barbara Carroll, Simon and Andrea Harrison, Marie Evanson, Ruth Crick, Ed Middleton, Dr Steven Powell, Natalie Moore, Sam Gamble, Maddy Templeman and Bob Stone. Also to my brothers, Alan, Paul and Nick Taylor and my beloved aunties, Shirley, Winnie and Ann. I also want to thank my COLC crew (you know who you are!), the Lakeside Runners and Go Run Birkdale. Your friendship and support have been invaluable to me; I love you all! To anyone I haven't named but should have, I'm sorry for my brain fog.

# CHAPTER ONE

## *London, October 1814*

The storm had raged all night. Summer's easy warmth had been pushed aside by autumn's fury and Percy Shelley's thunderous mood hadn't made it any calmer.

'I cannot believe you have written such vitriol about an innocent child, Mary.' Percy's eyes flashed and the red of his cheeks perfectly matched the red of his handkerchief that he now used to dab at his forehead. 'I did not imagine you capable of such cruelty.'

Mary Wollstonecraft Godwin bit her lip, waiting for the tempest to pass, as it always did. She had to admit, writing such sardonic comments about the birth of Percy's son in her journal had not been her finest hour. But since Percy had taken to writing in his own journal, rather than sharing one with her, she had imagined her words to be secret. It appeared not. Her own baby moved inside her, clearly uncomfortable with the raised voices. Mary put her hand to her stomach, hoping to soothe it.

'Claire? Claire!' Percy shouted into the hallway. 'Did you know about this?'

Mary sighed. Of course her stepsister Claire knew about it. Sly comments about Harriet Shelley were one of their few shared pleasures, and Mary knew that Claire's own journal was equally laced with acerbic comments.

'What is it, Percy?' Claire asked, taking a seat next to Mary on the sofa. She felt relieved at the unexpected gesture of kinship.

'It is this…' He stabbed at the journal.

Claire held out her hand. 'Let me see that, Percy.' Once it was in her hand, she cleared her throat and read aloud. '"Shelley writes a number of circular letters on this event which ought to be ushered in with the ringing of bells, for it is the son of his wife."' Claire looked up. 'Is this the offending line? I do not see the problem. Surely the entry is declaring the birth to be a joyous event that should be celebrated? A rightful son and heir — isn't that what the Shelley family desired?'

'It is a spiteful dig at Harriet, my son Charles, and myself. It belittles all of my philosophies and undermines my actions in one hateful scratch.'

'I think you are reading too much into it, dear Percy,' Claire replied. 'In fact, I know you to be misinterpreting it wildly and adding intentions to the words that the author never dreamed of. How do I know this? Because I wrote it, not Mary.'

Percy gasped and Mary threw a surprised glance in Claire's direction.

'If that is the case, then I apologise for my lack of judgement. I am very weary and —' he sighed heavily — 'events are taking their toll. I am going for a walk to clear my head.'

'Are you taking your boat?' Claire asked.

'Yes, I was thinking of taking it to Richmond Park. I do not suppose that you are in the humour for an evening stroll, Mary?'

Fury rose like a fire in her throat. Percy had been quick to anger when he thought the words were hers, but calm and ready to forgive once their 'true' author was revealed. Claire could be easily forgiven, but Mary could not? It made her angry to think of the congratulations passed to him on the birth of his son, all praise ignoring the swelling in her own stomach.

'No, Percy. I am tired and hungry. I need to rest and eat.'

Percy's face darkened. 'Well, I shall be away then. I will be back later.'

'May I come with you?' Claire asked. 'The rain has stopped, and the air is always so fresh and revitalising after a magnificent storm.'

Percy shrugged. 'If you wish. I will fetch my boat and then we can go.'

Once Percy had left the room, Claire took Mary's hands. 'You mustn't be so angry with him, Mary. You will push him away if you continue with this icy demeanour. He doubts your affection, and snipes like those in your journal will not help to convince him otherwise.' Claire had whispered the last, but the words still stung.

Percy returned, clutching a small paper boat. He looked like a schoolboy. 'Are we ready, Claire?' The lines at the corners of his eyes revealed the effort it took him to sound enthusiastic.

'Yes, Percy, let us away and see what adventures our burning boat brings.'

As they left the room, Percy glanced back at Mary with a mournful expression that made Mary's chest tighten. Never mind burning boats; Mary was worried that she had burned her bridges with the man she loved.

The view from the top of Richmond Hill was staggering; the town shrank beneath it while the hills swelled majestically. Autumn was reluctantly handing over its crown to winter, yet the leaves still clung to the trees and there was no sign of frost in the air. Percy gently placed the boat in the water, cupping his hand as he struck a match and sparked the flame. It reminded Claire of a baptism and a sacrifice. She watched while the boat hesitated before choosing a direction, meandering down the river towards the woodland.

Percy sighed. 'I am in no mood to chase the shadows of a passion tonight, Claire. Let the boat burn itself out in the Thames. I will see you back at home.'

He strode off without telling her where he was going. Claire was clearly not invited.

'Very well,' Claire murmured to herself. She swallowed her rising fear at being left alone in the creeping dark. 'I shall be captain and celebrant this evening.'

The cold pricked at her neck as she picked up her skirts and trudged over the damp grass. She walked past concealed couples and those on the periphery of rowdy behaviour, conscious of the impropriety of being a woman walking alone at night. Inwardly, she cursed Percy for his lack of care and for putting her in this situation; but unlike Mary, she would never take him to task for his behaviour. She had determined that her role, if she were to have any role at all, was to walk invisibly alongside them, nothing more than Mary's shadow. Her place within their household had teetered on a knife-edge ever since their return from Paris, and Claire knew that she must tread carefully.

It was quieter now, without birdsong. Fire had ravaged the boat's sails, which bent backwards like an outstretched arm skimming the water. Surely it would not sail much farther. Without Percy, it was quite a dull pastime. Claire had jumped at the chance to be with him; she'd had no intention of being the only ship's mate.

The boat curved an unsteady path towards an island dense with woodland. The boat was nothing but a fireball now, burning furiously towards its final destination. Claire fought the urge to call it back like a dog, content with watching its slow, fiery destruction.

A noise from the island told her she was not alone and Claire darted back into the shadow of some trees. As she watched, the moon partially illuminated the scene. She could see two figures in close proximity, but the distance and the darkness made it impossible to tell if they were in an embrace or a fight. Raised voices pierced the air, chasing away all thoughts of retrieving the boat. As Percy had said, the river could have it. As her eyes adjusted to the gloom, she could see the figures more clearly. A man and a woman with long blonde hair. His body leant over hers, casting hers in heavy shadow. Did he have his hands around her throat? A shoe fell from the woman's foot, hitting the ground just moments before her body did the same. The man stepped back, his shoulders hunched and his chest heaving as if he'd undertaken some heavy manual chore.

Claire gasped. Too late, her hand came up to her mouth to prevent the sound escaping.

The man turned, looking to locate the source of the noise.

Claire stepped back into the shadows, grateful for the cover of the trees. The man's face was pale in the moonlight, but she saw a pair of dark, sunken eyes and a mouth twisted upwards in an expression of intolerable cruelty. Claire's pulse quickened.

As the man turned back towards the body, Claire ran as quickly as she could towards the safety of the park's entrance.

She did not stop running until she reached the corner of Church Terrace. She had never been so glad to see the dirty doorstep and rotting window frames of their lodgings. Only the wind had given chase and propelled her at a speed her own fear had matched. Her hand was shaking too violently to put the key in the lock, so she banged on the door with her palm, not caring if she angered their landlady. When Mary opened the door, Claire practically fell into the hallway.

'Claire? What on earth is the matter? Where is Percy?' Mary's face was set with concern as she looked past Claire and into the street beyond.

'Close the door, Mary,' said Claire, battling to slow her breathing. This was no time for politeness. Mary did as she was bid, and Claire walked up the stairs and stepped into their rooms, snuffing out the lantern and standing by the window in the now dark room.

'Come and sit down,' Mary soothed. 'I will fetch you some brandy — if Percy has not taken it all.'

Mary returned with a small glass. Claire tipped it back, the spirit burning her throat.

'Tell me, what has happened?' urged Mary.

Claire put a hand to her chest and breathed deeply in the silent darkness. 'Oh, Mary. You will not believe what has just happened.'

'I cannot make a judgement on it until you tell me what it is,' Mary replied. 'And where is Percy?'

'He was in no humour to watch a burning boat, so he left me at Richmond Park.'

Mary gasped. 'Alone?'

'Yes,' Claire replied. 'But had I not been alone, I would not have followed the boat. And had I not followed the boat, then I would not have witnessed a murder.'

'Are you sure that is what you saw, Claire? Might it not have been a couple in the throes of a romantic interlude?' Mary asked.

Claire shook her head vigorously. 'I know what I saw, Mary. When the woman fell to the ground, it wasn't in a swoon, it was because the life had been strangled out of her.'

Mary exhaled slowly, gathering her thoughts. 'We will go back to the scene of the crime.' She clapped her hands together decisively.

'No!' Claire cried. 'I am not going back there. What if he is waiting for me? I saw him, Mary. I saw his face, and he may have seen mine.'

Mary cast a glance at Claire's hands knotted in front of her; they were still shaking. She walked over to the window; the night had swept in quickly. Even if the man was still at the park, the darkness would make it almost impossible to see anything.

'We will wait for Percy.' Mary sat back down. 'Did he give you no sign of where he was going?'

'None other than telling me he had no taste for sailing.'

'I expect he's gone to Harriet.' Mary crossed her arms. He always went back to Harriet. It was bad enough to have discovered that Harriet had paid the excess on their voyage back to London; knowing that Percy went cap in hand to his wife every time he hit a financially tight spot was just too much.

'Has he seen the baby yet?' Claire asked.

'Not that I am aware, but as Percy does not keep me abreast of his whereabouts, I have no way of knowing.' Mary's own baby shifted inside her, talk of Mrs Shelley and the new child making it as uncomfortable as it made Mary. 'Let us talk of more interesting things. Your murder, perhaps?'

'*My* murder?' Claire stammered, her face white with horror.

'Oh, goodness no,' said Mary quickly. 'Not *your* murder. I meant the murder that you have witnessed. Did you say you saw the man who committed it?'

Claire nodded.

'Then while we wait for Percy, why don't you describe him to me and I will do my best to sketch a likeness?' Mary crossed the room and searched the desk for paper and a pencil.

Percy's possessions dominated their two rooms. His effects littered every surface — books, quills with broken nibs, scores of stanzas in various states of completion, inkpots, handkerchiefs. Everything told the world that he was here, and this was his space. There was very little room left for Mary and Claire. Mary wondered if there would be any space at all for the baby.

'Perhaps,' said Claire, taking the paper and pencil from Mary, 'it might be better if I sketch the likeness. I see him so clearly in my mind's eye that it might offer some respite to move him to the page.'

Mary knew that was her stepsister's diplomatic way of asserting her superior sketching skills, but she wasn't about to argue; she had offered the suggestion merely as a way of steering the conversation away from Harriet, and it had achieved its aim. The mantel clock chimed nine, and Mary's stomach let out a quiet rumble.

'I will arrange some refreshments.'

It didn't take long to make the tea and arrange the paltry biscuits on a plate. Mary put them down in front of Claire, who looked up for a moment with a mournful expression before picking one up and continuing her work. Mary calculated the number of biscuits that remained in the tin. What was preferable? To feed them well today and keep nothing for tomorrow, or to spread the meagre portions, so they at least had a little sustenance each day? Her pregnancy and hunger had stripped her of her youthful glow, but she held fast to her personal mantra when physical need eclipsed a philosophical one: *this is the life I chose*. She would only have one biscuit tonight.

She did not wish to disturb Claire while she was sketching, and she needed a distraction to take her mind off the plate of biscuits, so she picked up the book she was reading, *Academical Questions*, and focused on the page with renewed concentration. The words danced in front of her eyes and made her head ache, yet she persisted. She could not say that the arguments and counter-arguments were marking themselves on her brain, but they did succeed in distracting her from the increasingly angry murmurs from her stomach.

'There, this is him. I believe it to be quite an excellent likeness to take to the Bow Street Runners.' Claire held the paper up for Mary to see.

'That is a fine drawing,' Mary replied, 'but I fear that unless they witness a crime, the Runners have no interest in solving it. No, we will wait for Percy and tell him what you saw; then we shall go to Richmond Park together.'

Dawn arrived before Percy did. His attempts to open the door quietly were unnecessary, given that Mary and Claire had both fallen asleep in the sitting room. Upon hearing his key in the lock, Mary sprang to wakefulness, knocking the book off her knee.

'Morning, Mary.' His hair was wild and his eyes wilder. As he leant over to kiss her, she smelled the stale fumes of alcohol on his breath. Mary wrinkled her nose as he noticed the teapot and biscuits. 'Visitors?'

Mary shook her head. 'No, Percy, that was our supper and will be this evening's too, unless you have been out all night securing additional funds for us?' She tried and failed to keep the bitterness from her voice.

Percy shook his head, as if the efforts of finding money were wearisome beyond all measure. Mary knew that money could not be found at the bottom of a tankard. 'I have tried, but I have failed again, Mary.'

Claire stirred from the other chair. She stretched to life and when she opened her eyes, her face beamed at the sight of Percy. Mary's heart shrank, knowing that was how she used to look at him.

'Percy!' Her tone was as bright as her smile. Even though she had undergone the same hardships as Mary, they had not taken their toll on Claire. A quick stab of jealousy pierced Mary's ribs and she let out a hissed breath, clutching her side.

'Are you well, Mary? Is there anything I can do?' Percy put his arm around her and the smell of stale alcohol turned her stomach.

'I have a little nausea, Percy, that's all. Perhaps you could fetch me some tea? That will help to settle it.'

'Certainly.' He nodded. 'Claire, would you like some?'

'No, thank you, Percy.' She stood up. 'I will make the tea while Mary fills you in on the previous evening's entertainments. We waited up for you; that is why you find us here.'

As Claire made the tea, Mary turned to Percy. She was torn between the urge to scold him for his selfishness and her heart's desire for peace, to turn things back to how they had been six short months earlier. When he looked at her, she saw nothing but love reflected in his deep gaze. She could not taint it.

'What is it, Mary? What has happened?' asked Percy.

'Claire believes she witnessed a crime last night in Richmond Park, when she was following your burning boat down the river.'

Mary relayed the story as Claire had told it to her, but as Claire's delivery had been breathless and patchy, she had to ask Claire to fill in some gaps in terms of time and location. The light of day brought a calmness and clarity to her delivery, and Mary wrote down all the fresh details that Claire imparted. By the time they had finished their tea, Percy was entirely up to speed.

'I sketched this.' Claire passed him the drawing. 'It is a likeness of the man I saw.'

Percy took it and spent a few minutes staring at it from different angles, rotating it in his hands. Claire and Mary shot a bemused look at each other.

'What is it, Percy?' Claire ventured.

'It's nothing,' he replied, though his words were unconvincing, as he could not stop staring at the portrait. 'Shall we take a walk to Richmond Park? See if Claire can retrace her steps? We might even find a dead body before breakfast!' Percy was half up and out of his seat before they could stop him.

Mary sighed. 'It might make a better meal than those biscuits,' she replied.

Percy was quiet on the way to the park. Mary did not push it, but she knew there was something he did not wish to say in front of Claire. The early morning air was refreshing, and Mary breathed deeply. Though she could not live on fresh air alone, it certainly helped to sustain her. The park was already populated by courting couples taking a morning stroll and nannies pushing perambulators.

Mary liked the time between seasons best of all. In this space between autumn and winter, the world was preparing for stillness and reverie, for slowing down. It matched her own rhythms. She would reach her confinement just as the winter was ending; her body would prepare for its own rebirth just as the spring arrived.

'Are you visiting Skinner Street this afternoon?' Mary asked Claire. She could not bring herself to say "Father", as his behaviour was anything but fatherly.

'I was planning to, but now I feel afraid to walk alone.'

'I will walk with you,' Percy said, 'and I will come and escort you back home. You need not be alone.'

'Have you no other arrangements this afternoon?' Mary asked.

'Nothing that cannot wait until this evening.'

Mary sighed inwardly. Percy had been like a ghost these past few months. Their life was one long game of cat and mouse with his creditors. There was never enough money for good lodgings, or to put food on the table, but there was always money enough for evening entertainments. She shuddered to think of the bills he was accruing, and how they were expected to pay them.

'You are out again this evening?' she asked.

'Unhappily so, my sweet.' Percy pulled a sad face, as if it were something he did not wish to undertake and had no say in. Perhaps a career in politics could beckon yet. 'It is the Philosophical Society dinner, so I really must attend.'

Mary's mind raced back to the plate of biscuits they had left on the table; she hoped no mice had eaten them in their absence.

'Oh, that is regrettable.' Mary knew her tone was mocking, but she could not rein it in. The Philosophical Society meeting would come with a long evening of feasting on ideas, food, and drink; sometimes she really wished she were a man so she would be allowed to attend. Her stomach agreed with her. 'But you always come back full of ideas and philosophies, so we all benefit from it.' She smiled. Percy pulled her to him and kissed her on the cheek.

'There! That's where it was.' Claire pointed to a clearing a little way back from the river.

'How did you get over there?' Mary asked.

'There is a pathway here.' Claire indicated a subtle trail through the woodland. 'Come on.'

Claire was the first to go, followed by Percy, who offered a hand to help an uncertain Mary traverse the overgrown path. She smiled at Percy in gratitude as she gathered her dress and walked through the dewy grass.

The clearing was empty, nothing but trees and grass. 'Oh.' Claire's shoulders sank.

'Were you expecting to find a body here?' Percy asked playfully.

'No, of course not. But it does make me doubt what I saw yesterday evening.'

'Is it not possible that you saw two people in an act of love, Claire? Who had sought some secret place in which to have some privacy?'

Mary locked eyes with Percy, her thoughts on the times in which their passion had been stolen and secret. It brought fire to her senses; she knew he felt the same way.

'Let us look around. There must be some trace, some clue. Did you not say that her shoe fell?' Mary asked.

Percy shook his head. 'The murderer would have been sure to pick it up.' He pointed suddenly. 'Look! Can you see that indentation in the grass? That must be where the body fell.'

'So, if there are any clues to be found, they will be around here.' Mary turned her gaze from the ground to the trees, scanning their half-empty branches and mussing the patches of fallen leaves with her foot.

'Anything?' Percy asked. Mary shook her head.

'What is this?' Claire tugged at a branch. Mary and Percy watched as the tree shook noisily and surrendered the object. Claire held out her hand, revealing a long piece of material. It was orange, the same burnt orange as the leaves on the tree — the kind of thing, Mary thought, that would have been perfectly concealed by nightfall.

Mary examined the fabric carefully. 'It is a scarf,' she said.

'And a very fine one,' added Percy. 'It looks to be made of silk.'

'Do you think it belonged to the victim?' Claire asked.

'If it did, then it tells us they had money and taste,' said Mary.

When they arrived back at their lodgings, the landlady cast a disapproving glance at them as they said their good mornings and went up the stairs. Even approaching the building made Mary's heart sink, but she fortified herself with her mantra and the thought of the biscuit to come. She scooped one up from the plate before sinking onto the sofa, fatigue weighing her down.

# CHAPTER TWO

That afternoon, Percy walked Claire to Skinner Street as he'd promised, steeling himself for another conversation with William Godwin. Percy had long since regretted his earlier commitment to act as an investor in Mr Godwin's publishing company; he had only made the offer in the hope that it might lead, in the long term, to a relationship with Godwin's daughter, Mary. Had he known her enthusiasm for the elopement, it need not have cost him so dear — their attraction had been mutual and immediate and needed no coaxing or wooing. Now he felt like he was paying Godwin out of guilt. After all, he had absconded with two of the philosopher and novelist's daughters, and no amount of financial reparation would undo the damage to their reputations.

'Shelley,' Mr Godwin said stiffly as he opened the door, 'I am in need of a further one thousand pounds. Can you secure it on bond?'

Percy knew it wasn't a request. Godwin knew all there was to know about borrowing off future inheritance, and he was happily wheeling his way through Percy and Mary's future capital with no thought, or care, for the effect on his own daughter or grandchildren.

'I can try,' Percy replied.

'Do better than that.' Mr Godwin's jaw clenched. 'I have had to tolerate shame and dishonour at your hands; do not add bankruptcy to your list of failings.'

'I will return for Claire at four.' Percy nodded, walking back down the street without a backward glance.

He hesitated, uncertain whether to return to Church Terrace or go to the house of Harriet's elder sister, Eliza in Windsor; perhaps today might be the day that she would let him see his son. The thought lifted his spirits, but deep down he knew that today would just be another closed door and he didn't feel up to that dejection, so he went home instead.

'Thank goodness you have returned,' Mary said brightly, putting down her book. 'I do not think the baby is in the mood for Greek verbs.'

Percy smiled at her, but Mary saw the sorrow behind his smile.

'Come and sit with me, Percy. I wish to ask you something.'

She saw him hesitate. He was preparing himself for a battle he did not have the heart for. Mary's own heart ached. When had she become the enemy?

'I know that there is something you are not telling me,' she said.

Percy frowned. 'Not telling you? I don't understand.'

'About this.' Mary had placed Claire's drawing next to her. She drew it up and passed it to Percy, watching as his expression changed to one of relief.

'Oh, this. Yes, you're quite right. Very perceptive, Mary.'

'Thank you.' She didn't need to be told that she was perceptive, but she'd accept it as a compliment. 'Claire isn't here now; you can tell me what it is that troubles you.'

'Is there something in the countenance that is familiar to you, Mary? Can you honestly say that you have not seen this likeness before?'

Mary frowned. 'I do not know; do you mean in another picture or painting?'

'No, I mean in life. Look closely at the eyes, the jawline — do you not recognise him?'

Mary stared at the picture. 'No, I do not think I recognise him. But I presume that you do?'

'Yes, Mary. I am almost sure of it. That is my tailor!'

Twenty minutes later, Mary and Percy were walking down Savile Row, past the bustle of deliveries and customers. Mary stiffened self-consciously as women dressed in the height of fashion passed them, looking down their noses at Mary's out of mode attire. It was yet another reason why she preferred books and learning to society life; she never felt equipped for that, as if never quite in possession of the full rules of engagement.

'Are we nearly there?' she groaned; her calves burned with the exertion. All this walking was no fun on an empty stomach.

'Almost,' Percy chirped. Mary knew that could mean they had several more leagues to go; his enthusiasm was boundless. 'Quick, Mary, hide! There he is!'

Percy pushed her towards an abandoned cart, which was a poor attempt at concealment.

'What do you think, Mary? Is it him? The man in Claire's drawing?'

Mary squinted against the sunlight. The man was dressed in working trousers, a baggy shirt and a waistcoat, with a scarf tied around his neck. To her eye, he looked no different to the other men that milled around; all were dressed in the same working garb. There was nothing to distinguish him from any other. It was true, his hair was dark, and his eyes possessed the same dark blankness that Claire had brought to life in her drawing; but whether that was coincidence, or the skill of the artist's pencil, was open to debate. When he turned his head to talk to another man, she saw his hair was slightly longer than the fashionable style and it brushed the back of his collar.

'I don't know. He could be one of thousands of men in London. Claire's drawing has a faint look of Frederic Martin to it, too, so it is possible that he was also on her mind when she drew it.' Claire had formed an attachment to a young French playwright whilst they had been in Paris.

'Are you saying that she made it up?'

'No, I'm not saying that. But Claire does have rather a fertile imagination and a taste for the dramatic. I just think we need more proof.'

'Like what? Oh, he's gone. Come on.' Percy slid out from behind the cart and dusted himself off.

'I don't know. Perhaps she needs to … I don't know, get another look at the man.'

'Capital idea!' Percy grinned. 'Then I shall invite him to dine with us.'

'You will never get Clara to agree to such a scheme; she was scared out of her wits.' Mary pleaded with Percy to see sense, but she knew how stubborn he was when he got an idea into his head. She was hoping the use of Claire's affectionate nickname might soften his feelings.

'No, Mary, you are quite wrong. I think Claire would be delighted to solve a crime — another crime — and bring a criminal to justice, after our escapades with her in Paris.'

'But how do we know that a crime has even been committed? There isn't a body!'

Percy waved this away, as though it were irrelevant. 'Quick, Mary, let us strike while the iron is hot.'

Mary slowed down. If he was determined to undertake this madcap scheme, then it would be his undertaking alone. She wanted no part in it. He hadn't seemed to notice that she was no longer walking beside him. Instead she stepped back, watching as Percy continued talking to himself, punctuating his monologue with effusive hand gestures. He walked into the tailor's establishment and a salesman flew to him like an expectant bird, ushering him into a space to which Mary had no access. She sighed and cast her eye down the row of shops. She swallowed as the unmistakable figures of William Godwin and her stepmother, Mary Jane, walked towards her.

Her heart pounded. The sight of her father brought with it an affectionate tug on her heart, swiftly followed by the sudden ache of the severance of that link. She thought to dart back behind the cart, but instead she stood frozen to the spot. Their steps did not falter, nor did their gazes turn in her direction as they breezed past her, as if she were nothing more than a street urchin, someone to be ignored. All the years of love and kindness had been swept away. If her father still saw something of her mother, Mary, in her features, he did not show it: it seemed that her face was strange to him now, not something that brought warmth of sentiment. If they had crossed the road, at least that would have been some acknowledgement of her, a gesture of recognition; but this, their ability to erase her from their hearts and minds, was a cruelty she could not endure.

'Will you not speak to me, Papa?' Mary called after them, her words attracting the attention of everyone but them. 'Am I nothing to you now?'

Mr Godwin stopped, his back straight and unyielding. Mary Jane knitted her arm through his, determined to firm his resolve.

'Were we in your thoughts when you absconded with that … that … inconstant poet?' Mr Godwin turned towards her. The expression of anger on his face was a shock. Mary had only ever known him to be a mild-mannered man. 'You have chosen your family; it is not ours.'

Mary Jane looked back at Mary, her expression smug. There was nothing else to be said. The stares of the crowd had brought tears to Mary's eyes and a burning shame that crept up her body and found a home in her cheeks. Mary watched as the couple continued down the road. So much of her life was on the sidelines of others these days.

Percy emerged from the tailor's shop. 'It is all arranged; he will come to the Philosophical Society with me this evening. I shall bring him to our lodgings for drinks beforehand. That way, you do not have to concern yourself with trivial matters such as food.'

Percy smiled broadly, clearly delighted with his plan. *Inconstant poet.* Her father's words echoed in Mary's mind. Percy really thought he was doing her a favour, but if he *had* brought an extra guest for dinner, then at least there may have been a chance of a meal that was more substantial than a piece of bread or a couple of biscuits. She looked at him. His skin still glowed and his eyes were not sunken like hers; he wore none of the scars of their poverty, the symbol of her commitment to him.

'I shall collect Claire from Skinner Street,' he said, as they turned towards their lodgings. 'I will not tell her of my plan, and I trust I can rely on your silence, too? It requires the authenticity of her immediate response. Her first reaction will tell us if he is the murderer.'

'And what if he is?' Mary asked. 'What if, by introducing him to Claire, you are furnishing him with the one person who can point the finger at him? What makes you think that a man who has killed once will not kill again?'

Percy placed a hand on her shoulder. 'The path to truth is often a difficult one.' He kissed her on the cheek. 'I shall return within the hour. Please ensure our rooms are suitable for a guest.'

For the second time that day, Mary was frozen to the spot. Was she so denigrated in his esteem that he saw her as nothing more than a *domestile*? Where were the poems, the heartfelt declarations? Mary Jane had warned Mary that Percy would tire of her as quickly as he'd tired of Harriet, that her pregnancy would be nothing more than an excuse for him to cast his affections elsewhere. She had not believed her and had supposed her words to be nothing more than jealousy. Mary Jane could not possibly understand the depth of feeling that ran between them, that was infinite. But recent events had shifted Mary's perspective.

Mary opened the door and cast a wearied glance over the rooms. Her temples throbbed and she wanted nothing more than to wash the dust from her face and lie down. Reluctantly, she scooped up the books from the table and floor, arranging them into neat piles. She blew at the dusty surfaces and plumped the cushions on the sofa. Finally, she made the beds before sitting down. Her back ached with the exertion. There, that would suffice. If it did not meet Percy's exacting standards for such low lodgings, then he would have to clean the place himself.

She picked up her journal, re-read the words that had caused Percy such consternation the previous evening, and wondered if he had not used the journal as a convenient way to facilitate a temporary exit. He clearly found it difficult being in such cramped conditions, but he was the only one capable of elevating them. Mary slid the journal underneath her bed. There. Now no one would find it.

Claire's excited chatter filled the hallway, and soon she and Percy were back in the room.

'Oh, you've tidied up.' Claire giggled. 'Are you making a nest, Mary?' She nodded towards Mary's stomach. Mary held it protectively.

'No, I just do not wish to live like animals,' Mary replied, her gaze darting towards Percy. He cast his eyes down, not meeting hers. 'This is a tiny space for three; it will be impossible for four.'

'We will have moved again by the spring,' Percy replied, smiling brightly.

Mary knew that. They had already moved twice since their return to London in September. She had learnt more about bailiffs and moneylending in the past month than she had in her previous sixteen years. *This is the life I chose*, she reminded herself.

'Will you read to us this evening, Percy?' Claire asked. 'It has been such a long time since you did. Perhaps we might have some Shakespeare to prepare us for winter?'

'*The Winter's Tale*?' Percy replied.

Claire nodded. 'Yes, that would be splendid!'

'Unfortunately, I have a Philosophical Society meeting this evening, but I'm sure you can read it with Mary. Who knows, you might have much to talk about during my absence.'

Mary was on tenterhooks all afternoon. Now that the plan was set, she wanted nothing more than the tailor's visit to be over and done with. With any luck it would stop Percy from meddling, and perhaps give Claire a name to pass to Bow Street. Seven o'clock came, the hour of the tailor's arrival. Percy had determined that Mary would open the door to their rooms, so that he could observe Claire's reaction. Mary feared that if the tailor was a killer, and if he had seen Claire in the park, then his knowing where she lived would put her in considerable danger. It would put them *all* in danger.

Mary braced herself for the knock at the door. When it came, she opened it slowly. Their guest was dressed in smart breeches, a waistcoat and a long jacket, not dissimilar to Percy's. To see them together, one may have believed them to be young men of the same social class. Mary glanced at Claire. Whatever dramatic reaction Percy had been expecting, it had not materialised. There was no hint of fear in her expression. Mary felt a tremendous sense of relief.

'Claire, I do not believe you have met Mr Hobbs? He works at my tailor's and has a keen interest in philosophy.'

The stranger held out his hand to Claire. She took it and curtsied. 'It is very nice to make your acquaintance, Mr Hobbs.'

'You know Mary, of course? I have spoken to you many times about her.'

Mary nodded politely, her cheeks flushed with pleasure.

'I'm afraid I got my timings all wrong, Jeremy. We must be away to the meeting now, otherwise we will miss our supper!'

Mary's stomach rumbled at the idea of food. It had been another day of bread and biscuits for her; Claire would have been given tea at Skinner Street. Hunger scratched at her with desperate claws; if it carried on like this, she might have to do something rash like steal a piece of fruit from a market stall. But then she would be put in prison. She sighed. What was the hardship in exchanging one prison for another?

The gentlemen closed the door behind them, leaving Claire and Mary alone.

'Well, that was most strange,' said Claire.

'Oh yes, why so?' Mary tried to keep her tone light and even.

'Percy, bringing a gentleman here. It's hardly the place for visitors, is it? I would never dream of bringing people to this hovel!'

Mary was immediately annoyed. 'You were offered the chance to return to Skinner Street, and to become a governess. For you, Claire, the options have been endless.' Mary sank into a chair. 'I am stuck here. In a trap of my own making.'

'In a trap woven by love,' Claire replied. 'I would prefer a love-trap to the traps set by societal expectation.'

'Yes, well, a trap is a trap.' Mary shrugged, standing again to sort out her supper. She would not offer any to Claire.

'That man,' said Claire, following her, 'he had a look of the murderer, don't you think? Isn't it a coincidence that the one man Percy should bring back here shares the same features as the man in my picture?' She shook her head. 'Astounding.'

Mary raised an eyebrow. 'You know, don't you?'

'Know what, Mary?'

'That Percy brought him here to see if you recognised him as the murderer.'

'I knew he was up to something. He was like a fidgety toad all the way back from Skinner Street; he kept asking questions about the picture and was I sure about this detail, that detail…'

'The plan was all his. I told him it was foolish.'

Claire snorted. 'When does a plan being foolish ever stop a man from undertaking it?' This made Mary laugh, and the moment rolled over like a cloud. 'Seriously, though, did Percy not think of the danger he was bringing to our doorstep? What if Mr Hobbs *had* been the murderer? He may have recognised me. What then?'

Mary shrugged. Claire's concerns echoed her own. 'I suppose he thought he knew what he was doing,' she offered weakly. It was no excuse, and she knew it.

'But it does not bring us any further along in our investigations,' Claire replied.

'No,' Mary agreed. 'It doesn't.'

# CHAPTER THREE

It was another restless night for Mary. The emptiness at her side made her mind race. No prizes for guessing where Percy had staggered off to. He was spending more nights in Windsor outside Eliza's house than he was inside his own. Soon the London gossips would have something to say about it. She swung her legs out of bed, pulled the blanket around her shoulders and tiptoed into the other room, careful not to wake Claire.

Mary picked up one of Percy's poems, half-written — nothing more than a couple of stanzas. The words chased each other around the page like wild stallions; ideas were fragments, half-blown flowers without substance. There were traces of his earlier genius, but that was all they were, traces; his creativity inhabited the same fog that his mind seemed possessed by — a fervent desire to see his son, to the detriment of every other feeling. It would not do. If she left now, she would be in Windsor by lunchtime; she might even see Percy on his return. There was no need to involve Claire in the plan. Besides, she needed her to be at home just in case Percy should come looking for her. She would leave a note saying she had gone for an early morning walk, and that she might call in on a friend before returning. Mary hastily scribbled the missive and left it next to a plate of biscuits to make sure it caught Claire's attention.

She closed the door behind her once she had readied herself for the journey and crept quietly out of the building. It reminded Mary of the summer's day on which she had crept out of her family's home on Skinner Street for the last time. Of course, she hadn't known it was the last time when she had left it. That morning, the air had seemed ripe with possibility. Now it had been replaced by a stagnant fug, with obstacles at every turn. London wore its poverty more openly than Paris; there was no nobility in depravity here, no stoicism, just street upon street filled with grimy people living gruelling lives. Mary was fast losing awareness of where their place in society was. They were rejected by polite society, shunned or forgotten about by those who, only months earlier, had called them friends. She was embarrassed that she could not name a single person who would welcome a visit from her. There was plenty of time to consider that on the walk.

The darkness clung to the sky and formations of birds prepared to depart for sunnier climes. Mary's solitary steps were slow and laboured and the baby wriggled its disapproval as the journey went on. Daylight came and as she walked further out of London, the number of greetings she received increased, lifting her spirits and strengthening her resolve to walk on. She reached Eliza's house at her predicted hour, but could not predict the welcome that awaited her. As she knocked on the door, she heard an upper window open. Stepping back in anticipation of making polite enquiries about Harriet, Mary was greeted with a full bucket of water. Her hat bowed like a sinking ship and her gown was drenched.

'Good morning, Eliza. Am I to assume that Harriet is not willing to see me?' she spluttered, water dripping from her hair.

'No, she will not see you! Get back to your harem.'

Eliza's angry expression and the curl of her lip bore more than a passing resemblance to Harriet. The two sisters certainly had their temper in common.

Mary sat down on the doorstep. 'It is no matter. I shall wait here until she does.'

'Then you shall have a long wait, for neither Harriet nor the baby are here, and they are not coming back either. They are getting as far away from that man as possible.'

If they were not here, then they must have been back in London, perhaps visiting Harriet's father. Mary groaned. It had been a long and wasted journey.

'When you speak to Harriet next, please tell her that Percy must see the baby, for all our sakes. It is driving him to distraction.'

'The only thing that drives Percy is the desire to spend the fortunes of others. That is the only reason he has ever come here. So, you'll forgive me if I politely decline to pass on your message to my sister. She has washed her hands of him, and now I have washed my hands of you. Good day.'

The window was closed with such force that the others shook in sympathy.

'Right.' Mary slapped her thighs, preparing for the long walk back. By the time she returned, it would be late afternoon, and she'd have wasted every scrap of light on this pointless endeavour. She had been foolish to think that Harriet would welcome her in. Sleepless nights, endless hunger, and worry about Percy had all taken their toll. She hadn't been thinking straight. She was in the very worst of circumstances and there was no sign of them getting better. At least in Paris their fortunes had been saved by the fee they had received for investigating the disappearance of Madame Lamont, but even that had not been enough to secure a moral standard of living. This wasn't living at all, and Mary's chest tightened at the thought of bringing her child into such a dire situation.

She plodded sullenly down the road, her head down to disguise the tears that now threatened to overwhelm her. Mary was glad that she was the only person around. It would do her good to unburden herself of this heavy emotional load she carried before she got back to Church Terrace and the unfriendly, watchful eyes of the landlady. They would be sure to move again before Christmas. Percy's modus operandi was to secure the rent for the first month, delay payment on the second, and then repeat the procedure as often as he could. London was a large place, and even reputations could be slow to travel. But although their poverty had escaped the common gossips, their living situation had titillated and fascinated people since September.

'Watch out!' a voice bellowed. Mary turned just as a horse loomed up. It caught her off guard and sent her fluttering backwards. 'I'm sorry,' a man's voice continued, 'I thought you would have heard the horse.'

'I was too preoccupied with my thoughts to hear you approach.'

'My apologies. Are you hurt?' The man jumped down from the horse and tied the reins to a tree. He looked down at her damp dress. 'Will you take a ride back to London? I am a medical student at the Royal College of Surgeons, but I can give you a ride to a coach?'

Mary coughed. A ride home would be infinitely preferable to having to walk there. 'I have walked from Church Terrace. Do you know it?'

'Yes, I was there with a patient just the other week.'

'You are a doctor?'

'Not quite.' The man smiled. He wasn't much taller than Mary and his youthful, open features decreed them to be almost equivalent in years. There was something instantly amenable about him that put Mary at ease. 'I am training to be a surgeon.'

Mary smiled. 'Then I should be delighted to accept a ride.'

'I was going to stop for tea; would you care to join me?' Mary's saviour had furnished her with his name and the details of his life on their journey. He was James Berry and training for the medical profession. He had one year to go before he qualified and he wished to specialise in surgery. 'I find riding so tiring.'

Mary, feeling a little nauseous from the enthusiastic motions of the horse, unused as she was to such a mode of transport, took her time in formulating a response.

'Yes, that would be lovely, if I had any money with which to pay for my own, but I do not, so I must decline.'

'You are my guest. It would insult me to take payment from you.' James smiled at her. His face hadn't quite moulded into masculinity and was peppered with the gentle curves of boyhood.

That settled, Mary clasped his waist as the horse cut through the countryside. Their journey completed in half the time it had taken her to walk, Mary was glad of the stern back of the chair and the warmth of the tea placed in front of her.

'I know it is not the hour for high tea, but I need refreshments. I take it you have no objection to my ordering them?'

Mary's stomach emitted a grateful rumble at the mention of food and she placed her scarf over it, hoping to muffle its appreciative chorus. 'I will endeavour to help you in your quest,' she replied, then went on, 'I am very interested in science. We seem to live in exciting times. Do you think we should ever be able to bring the dead back to life, Mr Berry?'

James laughed and placed a napkin on his lap. She had surprised him; it was a pleasant reminder that she still could.

'We are making significant inroads in surgery and science, but reanimation is a little beyond our reach just yet. Thank you.'

A stand of cakes and neatly cut sandwiches appeared on the table before them. Mary blinked at the sight of them, fearing them to be nothing more than a hallucinatory mirage caused by her hunger. She reached out tentatively, worried they might disappear at her touch.

'Would you like that one? And those sandwiches? I shall serve.'

James put the sandwiches and cakes on a plate and passed them to Mary. She fought the urge to cram them into her mouth quickly and loudly. The sugary hit of the cake sweetened her blood, and her heart pounded a warning that these weren't her usual habits; her body had got used to hunger just as her mind had accustomed itself to penury.

'It must be fascinating,' she continued, 'to read medicine, I mean.'

'Yes, it is,' James replied between mouthfuls of sandwich. 'Although it is a privilege I have fought for. I am not blessed with a title or family wealth.' He hesitated. The hesitation told Mary that the news of her relationship with Percy had reached even the educational establishments of the city. 'Forgive me.'

Mary gave a gentle laugh. 'I am fast learning that one cannot live off a title alone. I may have been born with a well-known name, but it does not aid my current situation.' She regretted the words as soon as she said them. Was she really so bereft of friends that she should seek kindness from a stranger?

'Forgive me. It is a very … trying time.' She turned her attention back to her plate, though her appetite had been replaced by the familiar nausea. Her body was a traitor — stubbornly refusing the opportunity to eat at the one time food was freely offered, yet crying out for food when there was none.

'Mary, would you and Shelley wish to dine with me? I took my degree in Edinburgh, so I do not know many people in London. It would be good to make some interesting friends.'

'I would hardly call myself interesting.' It was hard to be erudite and interesting when hunger gnawed away at you. 'But, yes, that would be splendid. Not tonight, though — Percy may have made other plans. Perhaps next Monday? He is at home most Mondays.'

'Next Monday it is, then.' James raised his teacup in Mary's direction.

'There is one additional request I must put to you, if I may?' Mary continued. 'We live with my stepsister, Claire. Might she come along to our evening's entertainment?'

'The more the merrier,' James declared.

'Splendid.' Mary smiled. The thought of a second meal focused her attentions back to this one. Hunger pushed aside the nausea and Mary picked up a sandwich.

It was four o'clock by the time Mary returned to Church Terrace. Percy was pacing up and down in front of the window in a manner that made her heart sink. When he saw her, he smiled and placed a hand on his chest. Mary took her time opening the door and hovered in the doorway, wanting to let him know how it felt to be frantic with worry.

'Mary, where have you been? You've been gone all day.' His voice was that of a stern parent.

Mary stifled a giggle. 'My apologies, I went to visit Harriet.' There was no point in lying, and even the long journey had not been enough to fabricate the name of a friend to whom she might have paid a visit. 'Is there a problem?'

'No problem — quite the opposite, in fact. I have secured us new lodgings. We must pack up and leave tonight. It is the only evening when the tiger does not prowl the cage.'

He meant the landlady. It was the evening that she went to visit her sister.

'Where are we to go?'

'Nelson Square,' Percy replied proudly.

Mary frowned. Nelson Square was nothing to be proud of, but compared to this place, it might seem like a palace. At least it looked respectable from the outside, though it would be impossible to appreciate the stuccoed doorways and sash windows at night.

'I have gathered all our belongings, with Claire's help.'

Claire smirked at Mary. Mary did not like the idea of Claire's hands rifling through her possessions. Luckily there were few to be handled, and certainly nothing secret or of any great import except her journal, but as Percy and Claire already used that as a source of entertainment when literary and philosophical works were scarce, that did not matter either.

On hearing the landlady's characteristic slam of the door, and safely under the veil of darkness, they bundled out of the house with the same luggage they had carried with them since departing London that summer. Mary's pregnancy gave her no immunity from transportation duties, though she was handed an oil lamp and Percy's precious rug to carry rather than the heavy trunk.

'The rooms were recommended to me by a gentleman from the Philosophical Society, Thomas Lillo,' said Percy as they set off through the London streets. 'He says they are the best rooms he has ever lodged in, and reasonably priced too.' He glanced at Mary. 'Perhaps the change of address, and scenery, will be of benefit to us all.'

Mary took a deep breath but said nothing. She would reserve judgement until she saw the rooms. Percy's optimism was a very becoming trait, but the counter side to that was a tendency towards spontaneity, pushing forward with sudden plans as and when they grabbed him rather than stopping to contemplate their long-term implications.

Mary shifted position. The oil lamp kept rubbing against her middle, and it was proving harder to walk on a full stomach than it had been on an empty one. She could have sworn that her stomach had swollen to double its size during the walk home from the tearooms. At least the baby was well fed.

She sighed. 'How much further is it?'

'Almost there,' was Percy's bright response. 'There is an iron railing in front, with gas lamps on the railing. I have secured our lodgings on the ground floor, so it will be like having our own mini moons outside the window. Ah, here we are.'

Percy dove into his pocket, pulled out a key, and opened the door. Mary looked up at the building: three storeys, a slated roof, patterned fanlights over the doorways — it certainly looked brighter than Church Terrace. She took note of the number, twenty-six, knowing it was highly likely that by the time she'd remembered the route back to the house, they would be on the move again. They stepped into the hallway. It had the same damp smell as all their previous dwellings. Mary stiffened as she prepared herself to look inside their rooms. At least their lodgings were bigger this time, with a separate space for Claire, but just like every other place they had lived in, all their amenities were crowded into a small area — a wash jug over an iron bath in the corner, a table with a couple of chairs in front of the window, one bed hugging the wall at the back.

'You are correct, Percy; the gas lamps outside are most pleasing,' said Claire. 'They will give you and Mary a deliciously golden light for evening reading.'

It was true, but Mary frowned. If they were illuminated all evening, then it would prove difficult to get to sleep. The light suddenly seemed a little too bright, the flames of the lamps a little too large. Mary spied the reason for their glare.

'There are no curtains at the window!' she cried.

# CHAPTER FOUR

A young boy in the rooms above had apparently been celebrating his birthday the night before. Mary hadn't known this from speaking to the boy in question but from his incessant banging of a kettle drum whilst padding across the floorboards above their heads, singing birthday greetings to himself for hours. Though it hadn't lasted all night, the noise had deprived Mary of any rest. She had yawned her way through most of the day, and only the thought of the meal at James Berry's lodgings had given her any pleasure.

Claire too seemed out of spirits and though she said nothing explicitly, Mary knew she was preoccupied with the events at Richmond Park. Mary felt a rising sense of guilt over not being able to help Claire in this matter, but with no body and no clue other than the scarf left at the scene, investigating further seemed impossible. There was no way of saying if the scarf was even relevant, short of going around every milliner and dress shop in London. A murder in a park was interesting — sheltered by the privacy of the trees and the stillness of night, but also exposed, public, with more than a little risk of being caught. What did that tell her about the murder? That it was not premeditated but a crime of passion? That the murderer was surprised by some unexpected comment or action from the victim that, in that moment, had been enough for them to squeeze the life out of them?

If so, then it must have been a relationship in which passions ran high. That could discount a marriage or a cohabitation, as domestic concerns would more effectively choke the life out of a relationship than a pair of powerful hands. Perhaps it was a

relationship that could only be conducted outside the home —
an inappropriate or adulterous relationship.

If she had gone with Percy to the park that night, then Claire
would never have witnessed the scene. Mary would have
allowed the boat to burn with no desire to chase its flaming
path through the water. Her lack of enthusiasm for Percy's
small passion had put Claire in this position, and that
knowledge knotted her stomach. She owed it to her sister to
put the matter to rest. A household steeped in melancholy was
not a welcoming environment for a baby.

Mary took the scarf out of the box in which Claire had
shoved it, along with the likeness of the murderer. The silk
slithered through her hands like a snake. A silk scarf of a bright
orange hue, too bright for her own subtle tastes but most
becoming on a woman with certain colouring. This was not the
scarf of a pale lady, nor one who wished to remain anonymous;
this was the scarf of someone bright, vivacious, carefree and
uninhabited — an external sign of a fiery, passionate spirit.
Mary ran with this wild scenario. The scarf had been a gift
from an admirer, but not a man of easy wealth who might go
straight to jewels or grand gestures. This scarf would be the gift
of a working man, a man with taste and knowledge of such
matters — a man who understood the differences between
tulle, silks and linen; who wanted the scarf to kiss the woman's
throat, to replicate the motions of his own lips. He intended
the scarf as a promise, not of matrimony, but of passionate
commitment. Mary cleared her throat.

All this was very imaginative, but it did not provide any real
clues as to the identity of either the murderer or victim. If the
woman was a working woman of a lower social class, then it
would be impossible to find out any more about her; people
appeared and disappeared in London all the time. *The Newgate*

*Calendar* was full of those who had come to London seeking work and wealth, and found vice and crime instead. Many were young and estranged from their families and quickly formed attachments that ultimately were unworthy of them. Often, they ended up on the streets, in the workhouse or in the debtors' prison — or as just one more body in the Thames. Mary surveyed her own surroundings; how easy it was for life to fall short of the standards one had expected.

Percy blustered into the room, interrupting her thoughts. He was followed closely by Claire.

'Pleasant walk?' Mary asked brightly.

'Yes, capital. I like the end of autumn. It feels like nature is in a fearful mood and takes out her anger on everyone with icy stares and harsh breath.'

Claire looked at him. Her blotchy cheeks and watery eyes showed all the consequences of the season but none of its beauty.

'And did you enjoy it, Claire?'

Claire rubbed her hands together. 'It was certainly chilly. I must remember to take my coat or else I will catch my death.'

'Right,' said Mary. 'Are we ready to go to dinner? James will be expecting us.'

Mary hoped that talking of James Berry might stir some latent jealousy in Percy, but so far, there had been none. He had been fascinated by Mary's discovery of a man training to be a surgeon, as he was as obsessed with science and anatomy as the rest of the modern world.

Percy had secured them a cab for the journey to Berry's lodgings. Mary lowered her head as she walked from the house to the carriage, feeling the eyes of the children playing on the street. The eyes were soon followed by tuts and titters and loud pronouncements mocking their perceived social class. Percy waved to the children, which sent them running in different directions, laughing as they went. Claire sniffed and pulled her shawl closer around her shoulders as she stepped into the carriage.

'I feel I have the beginnings of influenza.' She sniffed again, louder this time.

Mary fought the urge to roll her eyes. 'I am sure you will feel fortified after a good meal.'

'Speaking of which, did you remember to tell James that I do not eat meat?' Percy asked.

Mary bit her lip. Had she mentioned it? Percy's whims were as changeable as the wind; she felt certain that this was another one of them. 'I think I did, Percy. I apologise in advance if that turns out to not be the case.'

'Not to worry. As long as there are bread and vegetables, I shall feast like a king!'

Happily, there were. James had arranged a three-course dinner, which Mary could have wept at the sight of. As the soup was ladled out before them, James turned to Percy.

'I loved *Queen Mab*,' he said. 'What are you working on at present?'

'I started a romance, but I do not have the concentration for longer works; my mind flits and skitters. I can hold down an idea for an epic poem or a play in three acts, but that is about my limit.'

James nodded. Mary smiled at Percy's customary evasiveness when asked direct questions about his work. He was always working on something and nothing simultaneously. It took exceptional talent.

'Percy is trying to decide whether he should be a great philosopher or a great poet,' Mary said.

'Is it not possible to be both?' James frowned, looking from Mary to Percy. 'I mean, I am a man of science, so I know little of poetry, but I would have thought poetry and philosophy made good bedfellows?'

Claire tittered. Percy glared at her.

'In some ways they do, in the more theoretical ways; but just as you have committed yourself to surgery, I too must find my field.' Percy picked up his spoon. Mary knew that to be a clear sign that from his point of view, the topic of conversation was closed.

'And you, Claire? What is to be your future?' James turned his attention to Claire, who had picked up a bread roll. Mary watched Claire chew it hurriedly in order to answer the question before the conversation rolled on.

'My dream is for a utopian society of women. My ultimate dream would be a large house in which women of the same philosophy can live together harmoniously, without the harsh judgements and stifling expectations of society.'

Mary watched a flicker of something ignite in James's eyes.

'Really, Claire?' James leaned forward. 'I am most interested in this. Tell me more.'

Mary glanced at Percy; his lips were pinched into an expression of unease. Claire had taken his idea and was passing it off as her own.

'Yes, Claire, I too am very interested,' said Percy, picking off chunks of his roll and squeezing them into balls between his fingers. Mary braced herself for what was coming. 'Please, tell me about your … philosophy.'

The word philosophy was punctuated by a bread ball flicked from Percy's fingers. It landed in Claire's half-eaten soup. She fished it out with her spoon and put it on the side plate with no change to her expression. Mary didn't like it when their eyes met like this; there was a fire behind it that could easily ignite into passion. It made her feel discarded, as if she'd been chewed up and spat out like the sodden bread.

'My philosophy is your philosophy, Percy. I have merely adapted it for the fairer sex, for those of us to whom society does not wish to give a space, a home or a voice unless it is the voice of our fathers or husbands. It is easy to be you, with your title and your family's wealth.' Claire's voice shook, but there was no stopping her now. Mary put down her spoon. 'For a woman such as myself, with nothing — no breeding, no real father, and no money, society offers no opportunities other than to make myself amenable to men from a young age and secure a husband. Anything other than this is frowned upon. What happens to the woman who dares to contravene society's conventions? She is ostracised, thrown out. That is why I would like to create a utopia in which women and men are of equal value, with no gender distinctions at all.' Claire exhaled.

James Berry clapped his hands, his eyes wide with admiration. 'Well, Claire, you get my vote.'

'Unusual man, that Berry,' said Percy, as they started their long walk home. The carriage had only been a one-way indulgence. He had always intended for them to walk home after the meal — to "walk it off" as he'd so decorously put it. For Mary, who couldn't stop yawning, this was not a pleasing prospect.

'What do you mean, *unusual*? I think he is very noble and perfectly charming,' Mary replied.

Percy pouted. 'It is easy for a medical man to be noble and charming, but there isn't much poetry in his soul, which is odd, as he reminds me very much of my sister, Margaret.' He shook his head. 'I cannot think why.'

'Well, I liked him,' Claire replied.

'You like him because he seemed interested in your ideas,' Percy replied with a huff. 'I think he might wish to join your utopian society, you sold it so well to him.'

'He would be most welcome. He could teach the women how to become doctors and surgeons.' Claire sighed dreamily. 'Did you not find his conversation about dissection fascinating?'

'It interests me, but I have no stomach for it.' Percy shuddered. 'I once went to a lecture at which a scientist reanimated a dead frog's leg. Only its leg, though — it was twitching like a march hare.'

'Let us talk no more of dissection or other dark things — the night has shadows enough lurking in each corner,' Mary said.

'We shall continue our steps past the houses then and pray that the streetlamps are aflame. The nightwatchmen shall come to our rescue if the shadows spring to life.' Percy flapped his arms like a bat, first in Mary's direction and then Claire's. Both smacked his arms away and he shrieked with laughter.

'It is no laughing matter, Percy,' Claire scolded. 'You seem to have forgotten the horror I endured last week. I do not find it so easy to forget.'

Mary had done little but think about it. Her mind had whirled with possibilities and scenarios, sparked to life by their conversation over dinner and Berry's macabre tales of the operating table with its blood and sawdust. Nausea crept over her but was swept away by a sudden cold wind. She was grateful for it. If only the weather could take away all her ill humours.

'I have had some thoughts about your crime.' The words stumbled clumsily out of Mary's mouth before she could curb them. 'Sorry, you know what I mean. Anyhow, I think we underestimate the importance of the scarf. Perhaps the woman knew she was in danger and so draped the scarf on the branch of the tree as a clue to her identity.'

Percy shook his head. 'Not necessarily. It could simply have come loose in the quarrel — or even been used to strangle the victim?'

'Perhaps, but a scarf would leave other clues, would it not?' Mary tapped her finger against her lips. A scarf, if tied too tight around the neck, would surely have left marks on the skin. 'Bruises would surely be the mementoes, and they would look different to those made by bare hands.'

Claire started to shake and Mary shivered as well. To know that such violence lay in Richmond Park made an enemy of every street, transformed treasured landmarks into shadowy strangers and turned the once-familiar landscape into a most heinous villain.

'I'm sorry, Claire. I should have written down my thoughts and offered them in daylight, where they would not take such form.'

'The darkness gives shape to terrors but hides the detail,' Claire replied. 'I will have no nightmares from words, Mary, for I have been too well trained by Percy's ghost stories.'

'That reminds me, Claire,' said Percy, rubbing his hands together. 'Did I tell you the story about the sailor who was skinned —'

'No, you did not, Percy.' Claire's voice was firm. 'And if you attempt to tell me now, I will put my fingers in my ears and sing loudly and badly.'

Mary grinned. That was warning enough. Percy huffed, put his hands in his pockets and continued walking. She had only just got used to the path to Church Terrace; this journey back to Nelson Square was completely unknown. They seemed to have traversed every type of terrain the city could offer: damp fleets and sodden marshes lightly glazed with frost, pavements outside houses grander than anything she could imagine, and places that made her clutch Percy's hand a little tighter and pray for swift passage.

'Is our turn not that way, Percy?' Claire called out behind them.

'I am taking us a different way,' he replied.

Mary's insides tightened. She knew exactly where they were headed and knew that it had been a mistake to tell Percy that Harriet was not in Windsor with Eliza. How many times had he taken this route — the one that would lead straight to his father-in-law's house? Mary gritted her teeth. There would be no stopping him, and neither she nor Claire could ever guess at the path home from here. Even if they did, she did not want to contemplate the dangers they may face at this late hour. Night-time was the domain of thieves and ruffians, not respectable people. If only Percy had paid for a two-way carriage.

Arriving at their destination, Claire and Mary held back, standing under the branches of a poplar tree that hid Mary's burning cheeks and rising sense of shame. The house was grand, set back from the main path, with large windows on each side.

'Should I knock at the door? Or should I throw something at her window?'

Mary stiffened. She could picture Percy throwing stones up to Harriet's window when she had been on the receiving end of his fierce affections.

'No, Percy,' she replied. 'Come back tomorrow, during the daytime. It is late and they will all be abed.'

'We are here now, and I will not leave until I have seen my son.' Though he whispered the words, there was defiance in them. Mary was beset by an awful feeling that this would not end well. She could see it unravelling before them; Percy would gain nothing but reproach and increased bad feeling, which would turn him melancholy. She sighed. Why did he keep doing this to himself? Was it not enough that soon she would have a child and there was every possibility it would be another boy?

'Percy, come away from there, please,' Mary pleaded. She turned to Claire. 'See if you can get him to move away.'

'Your words have greater sway than mine,' Claire replied. 'If they cannot move him, nothing will.'

Mary sighed. She knew Claire was right, but her heart ached with helplessness. She could not stand and watch while he put himself in this position. Mary decided to take matters into her own hands, but she had only just stepped away from the tree and started walking towards Percy when she heard the sound of breaking glass. Instinctively, she shrank back under the branches. In moments Percy was beside her. Mary glared at him.

'Was that you?' she hissed. 'Have you just broken a window?'

'I might have…' He grimaced. 'What? It was an accident.'

A deep voice rang out. 'Is that you, Shelley? I have a gun in here, and if you do not get off my property, I will not hesitate to use it. I will count to ten.'

Percy strode towards the house. 'I wish to see Harriet and the baby. I will not leave until I have done so.'

Through the jagged pane of the broken window a baby's cries pierced the air. Percy walked towards the house, his arms outstretched. If he'd had a white handkerchief with him, he'd have waved that. Mary's heart was in her throat, panic making all sound impossible. Percy was walking towards a certain death with the swagger of a foolish man agreeing to a pointless duel.

'Percy, no!' Claire's voice pierced the air, a substitute for Mary's. 'May he not come in and see the infant? It is the only thing that will stop him.'

'A bullet will stop him.' The man's voice was sharp. The figure moved from the window. Mary's eyes widened.

'Percy!' She found her voice at last. 'He is going to get the gun. He will kill you! Please, come away from there. We will return another day. Let us write to Harriet and plead with her — we will beg on our knees if we have to. Please, come away.' Mary clutched her hands together.

There must have been something in her voice that spoke to Percy, as he turned to face her, shaking his head as if lifted from a trance. He rushed towards her, enveloping her in a long embrace.

'Mary!' he whispered, before collapsing into tears. He had never wept on her shoulder before. She held him tightly. He was grieving. There was something in this physical closeness that reminded Mary of their connection, and she was flooded with love for him. If she'd had the strength, she would have carried him all the way home.

Harriet's voice came from the house, softer than her father's but every bit as resolute. 'Do you hear that, Percy? That is the baby crying. He was asleep before your violent attack on the house. You may not see him, but you may hear him. That is Charles.' Mary looked up at the house. Harriet was holding the baby. Both looked so young and helpless, too fragile to generate such violent emotions in Percy.

'Percy, quick, there he is!' said Mary, but by the time Percy had torn his head away from her shoulder, they had gone.

# CHAPTER FIVE

'I must away, Mary.' Percy rubbed his eyes. 'I will return when the bells grant me immunity from the savage hounds.'

He meant the bailiffs and creditors hunting down his debts. Percy had been a terrified hare, trying to evade the hunters for the past three months. Mary sighed. At first, she'd thought there was something quite romantic about this love-in-idleness, where they were cocooned in their love against the rest of the world. But now her thoughts had changed, and Percy's declaration brought with it a sinking feeling in her stomach.

'You must do whatever needs to be done,' she replied, making a mental note to stock up on bread and biscuits before he absconded. 'But we must speak first. We never talk about our troubles anymore, Percy, and I fear that last night's events have sped up your decision.'

'As always, my dear, you know me better than I know myself and can sense the stormy tempests before I feel them.' Percy's shoulders slumped as he sat down. 'It is not being allowed to see Charles that is causing me distress, as if I am to be punished for falling in love!' His voice wavered. Mary smiled kindly, though guilt gnawed away at her. Had he never met her, had he never loved her, then perhaps a life with Harriet would have brought him contentment.

'I am sorry that our love has brought Harriet so much hurt, but I will never be sorry for our love, Percy.' She held his hands in hers and he kissed them.

'Bless you, Mary. Your words are always such tonic to me, and you are right — we could never mourn our souls' plight. But I want to see my son!' His voice trembled. Mary knew that was all there was to it; if he could see Charles, if only for a moment, it would soothe him far more than her words ever could. The Westbrooks had all proved insensible to this truth and were determined to keep Percy away. But the more they kept him away, the more adamant he became. It was a game of cat and mouse in which there were no winners.

The Westbrook house had not been so very far away, and Mary found it again with ease. It was a grand house. Mr Westbrook, Mary knew, owned several coffee shops on Grosvenor Square and did very well by them, though since Mary's pregnancy, the smell of coffee had turned her stomach. As she knocked on the door, her heart fluttered in her chest, and she prayed that Mr Westbrook would not be at home. She let out a sigh of relief when the door was opened by a housekeeper.

'Is Mrs Shelley at home?' Mary asked.

'I will just see if she is taking visitors. There was some trouble last night, and apparently the household was most disturbed.' The housekeeper scuttled away, returning a couple of moments later to usher Mary through to the morning room. She had not expected to be granted entry into the house, but then the housekeeper had not asked for her name. Had she given it, she might have received another pail of water.

'Mrs Shelley will not keep you long; she is attending to the baby. He was crying for most of the night.' The housekeeper tightened her lips. It was as if she couldn't stop herself from spilling all the household secrets.

'I cannot get him to settle, Mrs Dobbs. Perhaps you could try?' It was Harriet, the baby, Charles, restless in her arms.

'Perhaps I could try?' Mary ventured.

Harriet paled as she looked upon the face of her visitor. She hugged the baby closer to her. 'You!' she cried. 'Mrs Dobbs, did you let her in?' Harriet's voice shook with anger. Her eyes flashed and the baby wriggled in her arms, sensing the shift in her mood.

Mrs Dobbs looked between the two women; her brow furrowed and her lips a silent, straight line.

'Do you not know who this woman is?' Harriet spat. 'This is Mary Wollstonecraft Godwin or, as I believe she was calling herself in Paris, Mary Shelley. Not content with stealing my husband, she has stolen his name too.'

Mary held out her hands in a gesture of placation. 'Harriet, please. I do not blame you for scorning me, but your baby is innocent. Do not deprive him of a father's love.'

'And what of his daughter? Percy has shown no concern for Ianthe's wellbeing now that Charles has arrived!' Harriet barked. 'Typical of him to abandon the old in his constant search for the new. He will do it to you, you know. This grand passion you think he holds for you — he said all the same things to me. I imagine if we were to have tea and compare notes, we would discover that we have heard the same lines, delivered in the same way, destined to have the same effect. Well, clearly they have.' Harriet nodded at Mary's swollen stomach. Mary blushed. Never had society's judgement been so plainly exposed as through Harriet's gaze.

'Harriet, I understand what you are saying and you may be right. Percy is a poet; I am certain he falls in love a hundred times a day, and if he abandons me for another, well…' As she uttered the words, a cold sensation gripped her and Mary could feel the air leaving her body.

'Quick, Mrs Dobbs, help her to a chair. Fetch some water.' Harriet's voice was muffled and hazy, as if Mary were hearing it from underwater.

Hands pushed Mary down into a chair. She closed her eyes and put her hand to her forehead. A hand took hers and pressed a glass of water into it; her own shook so fiercely she struggled to grip it. Mary opened her eyes. Harriet was in front of her, all traces of her former anger replaced by unexpected concern.

'Here.' Harriet's hand was on top of hers, guiding the water to her lips.

Her senses drifted back into her body and the faint sniffles and cry of the baby flooded her ears. Harriet had passed Charles to Mrs Dobbs.

'Thank you for your kindness, Harriet. I do not deserve it,' Mary managed. 'I can see you are a person of natural tenderness; this cruelty you inflict upon Percy is not in your nature, and this bitterness will end only in more heartbreak. You can bring peace by letting him meet Charles. Please, give him the chance to be a father to his children.'

'He had no thought of being a father to them when he stopped being a husband to me.' A weariness laced Harriet's words.

Mary nodded; she could not argue with that. There had been glimpses of regret in those faraway trances of his that she'd found so poetic, but they had been but mere speckles. Her hand cradled her stomach, shielding her unborn child from Harriet's words.

Harriet held her gaze. There was steel to it but softness too; it took little to see that Harriet's wounds had not healed and her heart was still Shelley's.

'We are returning to Eliza's house at the end of the week. Perhaps he might call on us there.'

Mary felt the weight on her shoulders lift. 'Could you put that in writing? Then I may pretend we have had a note, rather than telling him…'

'That you came here and pleaded on his behalf?' Harriet snorted, the softness falling away and the shell hardening around her once more. Mary could see that it was the only means Harriet had of protecting her heart. She flung her hands in the air. 'Very well. If that is what it takes to be left in peace, I will write it now.'

As Harriet turned towards a bureau, Mary picked up the glass of water and sipped at it; it was no substitute for a meal.

'Here is your note.' Harriet handed her the envelope; it flapped like an irate bird. 'You have achieved your aim. Now, perhaps you will allow us to carry on with our day. I have not yet broken my fast.'

Mary stood up, knowing that the food that would break her fast would not compare to Harriet's. Her stomach grumbled. If Harriet had heard it, she paid no heed to it.

'Thank you.' Mary took the letter with a small nod. Perhaps, in different circumstances, they could have been friends, but there was no possibility of that while they were rivals for Percy's affections. Time would ease the pain and maybe they would find fresh harmony as they looked back on these fiery times with age and wisdom's softer focus. 'I will take my leave of you. It has been good to talk to you, and infinitely preferable to drink the water rather than be drenched with it.'

Harriet shrugged. 'Eliza is very protective of us.'

Mary nodded. She wondered if Claire would do the same for her. As she reached the door, Harriet spoke again.

'Mary, I apologise that your previous efforts to restore calm were met with such … hostility, but do not take advantage of my kindness. I have been hospitable today because I feel sorry for you, but I do not feel sorry for Percy. Let us not forget that his actions have brought us here. Take care of yourself, Mary.'

Mary nodded, smiled, and walked out of the house.

Once she had turned the corner away from the building, Mary looked at the envelope in her fingers — that open flap was tantalising. She shook the thought away and carried on walking.

Mary closed the front door on the children playing against the railings, but could still hear their tin cups clattering against the iron; the sound reverberated through her head. All was empty and quiet inside their lodgings. Percy had gone and every part of the space mourned his absence. He lingered in the half-written verses strewn across the table and in the book of philosophy with a folded page; but they could not bring him back, however much she might wish it.

Mary opened the cupboard to see a fresh loaf and a packet of biscuits. The urge to tear open the packet and stuff her mouth with biscuits to sweeten her sorrowful heart was strong. Instead, she picked out two biscuits and arranged them on a plate with a piece of bread and a curl of butter. Her baby rested calmly in her stomach; there was no sign of the defensive kicks and turns undertaken at Harriet's. Before she knew it, her hand was on the envelope and the yellow piece of paper it contained had been removed. Mary stared at the words written in Harriet's cursive and controlled hand; the handwriting belied the education she had received. It read: *Sunday, 12 o'clock, Eliza's house.*

The instructions shouted blankly from the page. Without adding the context, how would Mary explain their meaning to Percy without betraying her involvement? She couldn't. She slid the letter back into the envelope and placed it on the side.

It would wait as patiently for his return as she would. Picking up a book, Mary thought she might distract herself with some Greek verbs, but the words danced upon the page and no matter how sternly she stared them into place, they would not stay still. She threw the book aside.

From her vantage point, the outside railings reflected in the glass of the windows reminded her of a prison. Mary chewed her lip; without learning, literature, Percy or friends, there really was nothing to do but wait for the baby to be born. Mary huffed. Though society did not allow it, her instincts were the same as Percy's; she wanted to learn and to do things, not be silent and decorative and bored. Her role was that of a mother and housewife. No person with a brain in their head would wish to sweep floors or prepare meals without financial reward. To her mind, there was nothing more tedious. Happily, their want of food had not tested Mary's cooking abilities; her heart sighed for the days of someone else preparing her meals. She hated to admit it, but she was glad Claire had not returned to live with Papa and Mary Jane; Claire's companionship helped to fill the long days created by Percy's increased absences. Had Mary not known the cause of his disappearances, they might have seemed thrilling and given him an air of mystery and danger. In another time, he would have made a capital highwayman, but the people he was borrowing off often lacked his social standing and family wealth.

Without words, without love, how could she fill the long days until Sunday? The days rolled into one and usually she didn't stop to catch their names, so she had to concentrate to bring the day to mind. Thursday. It was Thursday. Did not James Berry say that he would be at the Royal College on Friday? Perhaps if she were to walk there, she might catch him and be taken for a cup of tea. That would be just the thing to calm her senses and revive her. She picked up her book again and this time the words behaved themselves, staying in their straight lines until Mary swept through them and onto the next page.

She was so wrapped up in the words that at first she did not hear the door open. When she did, she saw Claire's slight frame barge through it. Her eyes were wide with fright and her breathing was quick and shallow. Mary jumped up, guided Claire to the chair and fetched her a glass of water. Once Claire's colour and breath had returned to their regular state, Mary ventured to enquire about the cause of her distress.

'What has happened, Claire?' she asked.

Claire pointed towards the glass of water and Mary swiftly passed it over to her, watching as Claire gulped it down as if possessed of a tremendous thirst. Putting down the empty glass, she said, 'I think I have just been followed.'

'What? By whom? For how long?' Mary hadn't meant to utter so many questions, but they stacked on top of each other before she could stop them.

'I went back to Richmond Park. I thought it would be a good idea to revisit the park, seeing as how our investigation has stalled.'

Mary's cheeks flushed. She'd let Claire down. Her mind had been so preoccupied with Percy and the baby that she had not spared a thought for Claire's quiet desperation, or the impact of what she had seen.

'I am sorry for that. It is true, we have all been distracted of late and Percy has taken our attention, but I have not forgotten my pledge to you to solve the mystery and make you feel safe.'

'I do not feel safe now, Mary, and I do not feel safe here. How do I know that I have not been followed all the way back?'

Mary shook her head. 'Tell me what happened.'

'Well, after your mysterious early-morning departure and with no sign of Percy in the house, I felt at a loose end.'

'So you thought to yourself, "I know what I'll do, I'll take myself back to the scene of the crime and see if the murderer is lurking about"?' Mary folded her arms.

'Yes, that's about the size of it,' Claire replied defiantly. 'Anyway, I retraced my steps and went back, just in case there was anything we had not noticed the last time we went. I peered closely at the ground, much to the amusement of some larking boys who pointed at me as they passed.'

'And was there anything we missed?'

'No.' Claire shook her head. 'Sadly not. Even the earlier indentations in the ground had disappeared. Nature is wonderfully resourceful, isn't it? Able to spring back at a moment's notice. If only hearts were so resilient…' She had a faraway look on her face. Mary rifled through the list of possibilities in her mind before deciding on the recipient of that halcyon nostalgia — Frederic Martin, probably. 'I thought I was safe there, with it being broad daylight and swarming with people…'

Claire trailed off again, biting her lip. 'I suddenly had the feeling of being watched,' she went on, 'and it didn't come from the way the boys were making fun of me. In fact, I rather hoped they were still there so I could call for help if I needed to.'

Mary nodded and Claire continued with the story.

'The air seemed to change, without warning. An icy chill caught at my throat and I found it hard to catch my breath.'

Claire put her hand to her throat and Mary had to stop herself from rolling her eyes. 'The air was heavy with…'

'Winter?' Mary offered.

'No.' Claire shook her head. 'Murder.'

'Oh. What happened then?'

'There was a man watching me, half hidden by a tree. When I moved, he moved. I thought it was a shadow at first, but I held back and peered out from behind a tree, as if I were playing a childish game.'

'Go on,' Mary urged.

'Our eyes met and his expression hardened. Then he swept towards me as if he were flying.'

'What did you do?'

'I ran. Luck was on my side as he was slowed by several obstacles in his path. I ran through the park, out through the eastern side, with which I was unfamiliar. It is certainly hillier on that side…'

'Did you lose him?'

Claire nodded. 'In the park.' Then her brow furrowed. 'I am almost sure of it. I walked at a brisk pace all the way back, once I had regained my bearings.' She nodded at Mary. 'Where did you go, anyway?'

'Percy is hiding from his creditors again.' Mary sighed. 'He will not return until Sunday. I went to talk to Harriet, hoping she would let him meet the baby.'

'And? How did it go?'

'She has agreed to let him see the baby.'

'Finally.' Claire threw her arms into the air. 'That is good news. Perhaps now a great cloud will be lifted from him, and we can bring this murderer to justice before he comes for *me*.'

# CHAPTER SIX

The following morning Mary had awoken intending to pay a visit to Mrs Knapp, who used to work for her father before Mary Jane dismissed all of the staff he had had before their marriage. Mary had grown up with Mrs Knapp and was very fond of her, so she had kept up a correspondence with her and had been pleased to receive an invitation to come round and visit. Mrs Knapp was now a landlady, and Mary had determined that Claire should accompany her on a visit. The journey seemed like a hazy dream as the early morning mist turned buildings and market holders into shadows against the daylight. Claire was silent, her face set against greetings or gestures, ready to spring onto her heels at any moment, Mary mused, careful of any threat that might lurk within the shrouded streets.

Mary breathed deeply, struggling to match Claire's pace. Her stomach had lowered, giving her the sensation of carrying an increasingly heavy load, a pile of books, perhaps, that someone kept adding to until the weight sank lower and lower. She thought that before the end of the pregnancy, gravity would have pulled her so far forward that she would roll into places headfirst rather than walk into them.

'Can you slow down a little, Claire?' Mary asked. 'I cannot walk as quickly as you.'

'Sorry, Mary, I will walk alongside you. It is safer than speeding off alone, at any rate.' Claire's steps slowed to match Mary's.

'Did you get any sleep?' Mary asked.

'Happily, I did. I slept very well.'

'Perhaps now you have seen the man and confronted the fear, it has put an end to it?' Mary offered.

'No, Mary, that is not it at all.' Claire shook her head. 'But it has hardened my resolve in one matter.'

'Oh yes, and what is that?'

'Until the matter is concluded, and we have uncovered the truth, I will move back in with our parents.'

Mary caught her breath. 'You cannot leave me,' she stuttered. 'Certainly not to live with them. My reputation will be irrevocably shattered.'

Claire snorted; her features took on the same customary slyness that had possessed them when she'd told on Mary as a child.

'You are pregnant with Percy's child, he who has also just had another baby with his wife. His *wife*, Mary. Surely you are under no illusions that you have even the slightest shred of respectability in London? What do you care about such things, anyway?'

Mary inhaled; Claire had a point. She knew all too well that her reputation and social standing had remained ashore when she'd eloped with Percy to France. Now she was pregnant, there was no remedy. It irritated her that she even considered such matters.

'But with Percy's constant disappearances...' Her words faltered and were replaced by sudden tears.

Claire put an arm around her shoulder. 'Mary.' Her voice was softer now. 'This is the life you have, but it does not have to be my life. It does not even have to be yours either, if you don't wish for it. We could go away somewhere where we are not known and reputation cannot follow us — to Wales or Scotland — and take a cottage in a remote village where there are fish and birds and sea...'

Mary could almost smell the salty seawater. Anything sounded better than being left alone in noisy rooms, hiding from bailiffs, pleading with creditors, being desperate for food — a life of worry and deception.

Mary sighed. 'You paint a tempting picture, Claire. But my life is with Percy, and it always will be.' No matter what he had done, or how hard their life together had been, nothing had erased the love she felt for him.

'At some point, I will need to make a life of my own,' Claire countered. 'I cannot continue in my role of chaperone once the baby is here. I have already made enquiries into opportunities.'

Mary bristled. How could Claire even think of abandoning them? The devil on her shoulder reminded Mary that not three months earlier, this was what she had prayed for. What tricks the fates had played upon them. How quickly the tables had turned. She could not be left alone; she would beg not to be left alone if it came to it.

'I will not leave until Percy's financial arrangements are sorted,' Claire said finally.

That was consolation enough; it could take years.

'Perhaps we could try to get out of the house more during the day? Undertake our investigations by day and offer our conclusions by night?' Mary knew that the lure of solving the crime would prove too delicious a prospect for Claire to pass up.

'That sounds like an agreeable plan.' Claire stopped walking and held onto Mary's arm. 'But I intend to make alternative arrangements for the spring. Once the baby has arrived, there will be no space for me in your lodgings. I must find my own way.'

'It is almost time for the lectures at the Royal Institution.' Mary's eyes flashed with excitement. 'We can attend those. I am sure that James Berry would be delighted to accompany us if Percy is … otherwise engaged.'

'That would be splendid. It is good to keep our minds active when there is so much idleness.' Claire seemed much placated by Mary's words and they walked the rest of the journey with matching steps and easy hearts. A compromise had been reached that was satisfactory to both parties. Negotiating difficult situations and acting as mediator was becoming second nature to Mary now.

Mrs Knapp's lodgings were not grand. Mary and Claire stepped past women unfurling dirty rugs onto the path and children playing with broken bottles and shards of glass. Mary could not resist shouting out a warning as the children ran past, brown spikes of glass upturned like arrows, one in a hand scarcely big enough to carry it. Mary tutted, gently lifted the glass from the reluctant toddler and put it into her bag. The child frowned his disapproval before bursting into tears and running to catch up with the other children. Mary straightened and hurried to reach Mrs Knapp's house before the child reached his friends — not that the child would have the words to articulate the crime committed against him. If Mary and Percy did not sort out their finances, it could be their child in this peril. A stony fear passed over her. There was no way she would allow that to happen.

Mary knocked on the door. A dog barked behind it and Claire cowered behind Mary.

'Mary! Jane! What a pleasant surprise.' The woman had a wrinkled face and was dressed practically, wiping her hands on an apron as she greeted them. Small blue eyes shone with mischief and she smiled broadly. Mary returned the smile, grateful to see a friendly face. 'Come in, come in.'

The beast that had caused Claire such consternation came into view. It was long, thin and white, of indeterminate or possibly multiple breeds, and with a brown patch over its right eye. It sniffed at Claire and Mary, but its interest was soon diverted by a piece of raw meat that Mrs Knapp threw out of the door.

'It is good to see you both. Sit down, sit down.' She ushered them into the kitchen and onto chairs that were as thin as bones and equally easy to break. Mary lowered herself onto one slowly.

'I see you are expecting.' Mrs Knapp sniffed. 'Can't imagine Mr Godwin's too pleased about it.' The old woman laughed, exposing the gaps in her teeth.

Claire smiled. 'Mary is the talk of London. They say that Papa sold us to Percy for a thousand pounds. Can you imagine being worth that much?'

Mrs Knapp sniffed again. 'Mr Godwin has no head for money, Jane. He never did.'

'I'm known as Claire now,' Claire said.

'Claire? Why on earth have you changed your name?'

Mary stifled a laugh. Mrs Knapp had always been unflinchingly direct.

Claire shrugged. 'It is my middle name and I prefer it to Jane.'

Mary resolved that one day she would tell Mrs Knapp the full tale of Claire's obsession with Rousseau and how she'd changed her name to make it sound more romantic, the name of a heroine rather than a sidekick.

'You are looking very well, Mrs Knapp,' Mary said. 'How is life as a landlady?'

'Same as ever, same as ever.' Mrs Knapp shook her head. 'Chasing payments, people doing night-time flits, false names, unreliable staff…' The words trailed off into a disappointed sigh.

'Unreliable staff?'

'You know how it is; they come and they go. But enough about my woes — where are my manners? Tea, we must have tea.'

'Is there anything I can do to help?' Mary rose from the chair.

'How about buttering that bread?' Mrs Knapp pointed towards a loaf of bread and a dish of butter that made Mary's mouth water.

'Of course.' Mary smiled. 'You were saying you're having problems keeping staff?'

'Yes, I had a girl to help with the domestic chores; there's a lot to do in this business, you know.' Mrs Knapp paused. 'Shall we have some fruit as well? I haven't had breakfast yet.'

Mary's churning stomach reminded her that they hadn't either, and her heart leapt at the sight of Mrs Knapp walking over to the table, her arms laden with fruit and biscuits.

Once the tea was made and the bread sliced and buttered, they all sat down at the table. Mary's hunger intensified as she took in the delicious feast in front of them. 'What happened to the girl?' she asked, helping herself to an apple, a biscuit, and a thick slice of bread.

'What girl, dear?' Mrs Knapp poured the tea.

'The domestic help?' said Mary. 'You said that you were having difficulties with staff.'

'Oh, yes, that. I had a girl, Annie — very helpful she was, and then one night she was gone. Just upped and left.'

'She left?'

Mrs Knapp took a biscuit, nodding as she crunched it. 'Yes, but that's not the odd part.' She continued to crunch the biscuit. Mary willed her to hurry, but Mrs Knapp seemed to enjoy taking her time with it. The ticking of the clock battled with the crunching of the biscuit; both seemed to get louder as Mary waited. Mrs Knapp finally wiped her mouth. 'She just left without taking her things … most strange…'

'She left, taking nothing?' Mary asked. 'She took nothing at all?'

Mary and Claire exchanged a glance. A missing young woman. Could this possibly have something to do with what Claire had seen in Richmond Park?

'She sent her brother to collect her possessions a few days later.' Mrs Knapp shook her head. 'There was just something a bit off about him. He was all on edge and fidgety, like it was his guilt, not hers.'

Mary chewed over that last phrase. *Like it was his guilt, not hers.* How many young people came to London to seek employment? Mrs Knapp's lodging house was only one of hundreds of such houses crowded into undesirable districts. Mary supposed that if they visited all the places that employed young women, all would tell similar tales of night-time flits and sudden disappearances. London was a giant marsh; it could swallow you up and leave no trace of you behind.

'Can you describe what he looked like, the brother?' Claire asked.

'Dark hair and eyes, kind of stringy.' Mrs Knapp wrinkled her nose as if the description brought an unpleasant smell with it.

'Stringy?' Claire probed.

'Yes, not much meat on him, and tall. Actually, I recognised him. He's a local lad — works at the butcher's two streets over. Holland and Sons. He isn't a Holland, though.'

'Did he tell you where Annie had gone?'

'No, and I didn't ask. I'll get another girl in, if I can cope with all the drama that comes with them.'

Mary thought of the gathering dust on the surfaces in their rooms, the impossibility of conjuring up meals with no food and no money to buy it. She was almost tempted to apply for the job herself, or perhaps offer Claire up for the position.

'What was Annie's surname?'

'She told me it was Bell, but I don't know if that was her real name or one she'd plucked from the air.' Mrs Knapp folded her arms. 'Why are you so interested in this?'

They told Mrs Knapp the entire story and her interest was immediately piqued. Shortly afterwards, they made their way towards the shops. Mrs Knapp was no substitute for Percy; she did not walk with a light gait and poetic air, but she knew everybody and they either raised a hand in greeting or shrank back into a doorway at the sight of her. In no time at all, they had reached the butcher's and as the door opened to let a customer out, the pungent aroma of blood and flesh invaded Mary's nostrils. Nausea swept through her.

'I think I will wait outside.' She held her hand to her nose. It was disappointing not to go in, but her body was grateful to stay in the cold, meat-free air.

Mary stared at the waxy carcases of the pigs that hung in the window. Just looking at them made her stomach turn. Perhaps Percy was right in his vegetarianism. She shuddered at the thought that these were once living things and closed her eyes tightly. When she opened them again, she could see that Claire and Mrs Knapp were speaking to a man behind the counter.

He was shaking his head and pointing to an unspecified point in the distance. Claire and Mrs Knapp left the shop.

'Well, did you find him?' asked Mary.

'Day off,' said Mrs Knapp.

'What was the man pointing towards?'

'Thomas's lodgings. Very helpful he was — he presumed young Thomas Bell owed me money.' Mrs Knapp laughed. 'Sometimes it pays to have a reputation.'

Mary could not help but agree. Mrs Knapp had been a stern enough housekeeper; heaven only knew what she'd be capable of as a landlady.

They stepped away from the shops, criss-crossing the street until they reached a rundown building tucked back from the others. Broken windows and badly patched areas where brickwork no longer met wooden frames told Mary that this wasn't the sort of place she'd want to visit alone, or at night, and she was glad of Mrs Knapp's formidable presence.

'There it is.' Mrs Knapp hitched her skirts and strode over to the building. Claire and Mary looked at each other, sharing raised eyebrows and terrified glances. Together they walked towards Mrs Knapp, who was pounding forcefully on a door.

'Thomas Bell, I know you are in there. Open this door or it's the debtors' prison for you!' Mrs Knapp bellowed, before turning towards Mary and Claire with a wink.

A chorus of unseen dogs barked, but the door remained stubbornly closed. Mrs Knapp pounded again, and a curtain twitched at the top window, the only sign of life the building was willing to share. Mary frowned. Perhaps the butcher had got the address wrong? Surely the only inhabitants here were of the animal kind.

'I mean it, Thomas Bell! You open this door at once or it's the bailiffs!'

The sound of footsteps running down wooden stairs thundered through the fragile building, making the windows shake. A door swung open and a face appeared.

'Mrs Knapp!' The young man put a hand to his chest and exhaled loudly. 'Was that you shouting about bailiffs and debtors' prisons? I am not in any debt to you…'

Mary frowned. His choice of words was interesting. *Not in any debt to you*, meaning he may have debts elsewhere. Mrs Knapp's threats had clearly struck a chord with him.

Claire was observing him closely. Mary could see she was trying to compare his features with those of the man she had seen in the park. But there was nothing but a faint curiosity in Claire's gaze. Mary resigned herself to another dead end.

'Can we come in? I have a couple of questions for you,' Mrs Knapp said.

'Questions? What are you, the Bow Street Runners? I didn't know they were taking on women.' Thomas laughed. 'Come in, by all means, but I was not expecting visitors and I've given my valet the day off.' He grinned, revealing a row of rotten teeth.

The staircase wobbled as they ascended it, the rail rotten and exposed. Mary took tentative steps. By the time they reached the top of the building, sweat had broken out on her forehead.

'Welcome to my humble abode!' Thomas held out a hand, presenting the room.

Mary looked around. The cramped room made their own lodgings look palatial. It was dark and smelt of tobacco, which scarcely disguised the dank undertone of mould beneath it. Almost every surface was littered with clothes, papers and wrappers, as if to compensate for the room's sparseness. A makeshift bed was sprawled on the floor amongst the mess.

'You live here?' Mary asked, before she could stop herself.

Thomas sniffed. 'No money, no choice.' Mary felt a swell of sympathy for him. She had only had a taste of poverty; she was lucky to have never been fully immersed in it like this young man.

'I've seen you before, haven't I?' Claire said at last. Her voice was firm and confident, not the voice of someone facing a foe. 'You followed me out of the park?'

Thomas scratched his head. 'I … er … wasn't following you… I mean, I was, but I didn't mean you any harm. I was trying to introduce myself to you, but when I saw you up close — so to speak — I saw you would never give a man like me the time of day. You gave me such a look too, and then you ran away.' He shrugged.

Mary glanced at Claire. Was this likely? Had he just been trying to talk to her, or was this a cunning attempt to justify his actions?

'I might have walked with you awhile…' Claire replied. Mrs Knapp and Mary raised their eyebrows. 'But a woman should not walk alone in the park without a chaperone for protection — I knew I was putting myself in danger by being there.'

'If we had walked together, you could have said I was your brother. Our looks are not altogether dissimilar. Do you always go to Richmond Park? Perhaps we might walk there together on Monday — that's my half-day.'

Claire flinched at the comparison; Mary knew she would be appalled by anyone making that assumption.

'Very well. What time shall we say?'

Mary looked at Claire. What was she up to?

'One o'clock.' Thomas's rotten grin widened.

'One o'clock it is. I will meet you on the bench at the entrance to the park.' Claire nodded decisively, then turned to

Mary and Mrs Knapp. 'I think we have everything we need. Shall we go?'

Mary and Mrs Knapp were so bemused, they simply nodded and began to descend the rickety stairs. As they walked, something small and furry darted past them.

'What in the name of all that is holy was that?' shrieked Mrs Knapp.

'Oh, that's just the cat. It sees off the vermin,' replied Thomas, throwing a wink back towards Claire, who was at the rear of the group.

'That was no house cat — that was a giant rat!' Mrs Knapp shook her head. Thomas laughed and he and Mrs Knapp fell into walking together, discussing the size of cats and London's problems with sewage and vermin. Mary and Claire held back.

'What do you think you're doing, agreeing to walk out with him, Claire?' whispered Mary.

'I agreed because —' Claire pulled something from the folds of her dress — 'while his back was turned, I picked up this.' She unfurled an orange scarf, which blew out like a gentle wave in front of her.

Mary frowned. 'Is that the scarf we found at the park?'

'No,' Claire replied. 'But it is very similar, which tells us that Thomas Bell might know more about this than he is letting on.'

# CHAPTER SEVEN

On Friday Mary paced up and down outside the Royal College, desperately trying to dodge the coughs and splutters of people who passed. At midday, a group of medical students came out, their tailcoats and high jinks contrasting violently with the ailing and infirm going in. James Berry was in the thick of them, laughing and punching the arm of a fellow student who had doubtless made some wildly inappropriate jest.

'Miss Godwin!' James smiled as he saw her. He allowed the rest of his group to fall away, proclaiming that he would catch up with them later. Mary's cheeks reddened. She had almost forgotten her actual name, and it seemed odd to hear it from a new friend's lips, as if it no longer belonged to the pregnant woman who owned it. 'How delightful to see you. Are you in a mind for luncheon? I am ravenous.'

'And what delights have you been learning about this morning?' she asked. They stepped into a peaceful rhythm, their strides and smiles equally paced.

'We are studying anatomy this term. This morning, we were learning about surgical procedures.'

Mary's eyes widened. 'That sounds fascinating. You can tell me more about it over tea and I shall tell you of our adventures.'

'Capital!' James rubbed his hands together. 'It has made my day seeing you, Mary, it really has.'

As James's friends disappeared into a coffee house on Grosvenor Square, Mary relaxed. A gentleman would never take a lady to a coffee house; they were male terrain, and any women who went there risked garnering the most unsavoury reputation. The baby kicked a reminder that Mary was in no position to talk about reputations, yet here she was again, out in the middle of the day with another man. Mary Jane would have a field day. Mary still felt the restraints of expectation, even though she had severed their cords.

'Here, I think. They do a capital fish.'

Mary's stomach turned at the word, but she smiled meekly and nodded acquiescence, and they walked into the restaurant. The air was busy with the clink of bone china and the aroma of homely meals that made Mary's heart swell. Nothing was more conducive to good spirits than a cup of tea. Soon they were seated with no fanfare or judgemental gazes, and Mary felt almost proud to be sitting in the chair. Orders were taken and tea brought with impressive swiftness. Once the tea was poured, they fell into conversation.

'Tell me, Mary, about your adventures.'

'I have actually found myself caught up in a curious incident involving a missing person or a missing body, or both.'

James leaned forward. 'Go on.'

'Firstly, Claire thought she had witnessed a murder in Richmond Park, but when we returned to the scene the body had disappeared. Then, through an encounter with a woman who used to work for my father, we have somehow become involved in the disappearance of a servant.'

'That makes my days seem most uneventful.' James smiled.

'It appears almost impossible to find leads on either in London.'

'I suppose it is because there are so many places to hide oneself or for a body to be hidden or disposed of.'

'I fear you might be right.' Mary sighed. 'It feels like we are looking for a needle in a very large haystack.'

'If anyone is up to the challenge, then it's you.' James smiled brightly. Mary tried to smile back, but a sudden awareness of how her behaviour might be interpreted came over her and her mouth twitched awkwardly. It was strange, but she had fallen into a grateful friendship headlong, with no real thought of social conventions or anything other than easing the loneliness that gnawed away at her — the great swelling boredom that clouded her days and worsened when Percy wasn't there. Did she see James as some sort of substitute for Percy? It hadn't been her intention and there had been no sign of anything other than friendship from him; hadn't he invited them all to dine, including Percy? Those were not the actions of someone intending a clandestine romance.

'I must admit,' she said, 'that much as I like to protest to Claire about our investigations, I find them rather thrilling.'

'What is your next step?' James asked.

'Claire has met a man who she thinks has some connection with it. They are going for a walk on Monday afternoon to Richmond Park.'

'Richmond Park?' James frowned. 'The scene of the crime? Does Claire not worry that she may place herself in the greatest of dangers by going there?' He clicked his fingers. 'She shall not go alone — we will go and we will keep watch over Miss Clairmont. We shall ensure her safety.'

Mary smiled as relief spread through her. Here was a man who could empathise with others, who could see where help was needed and offer assistance without being asked for it. Percy had more sympathy for animals than people and often only saw his own concerns and never how they might impact on others. It was good to have a friend like James.

'If you are sure it is not an inconvenience to you?'

'Not at all. I am going to spend the day with books on Monday. I do not think they will tell on me if I take a little stroll in the park, will they?'

When Monday came, it brought doubt and fear along with another morning mist. Claire paced around the room, besieged with nerves that quickened her pace and her tongue.

'I mean, what if Thomas tries to drag me over to the island and kill me?' Claire gulped.

'Claire,' Mary soothed, 'he thinks he is to be your paramour. He is not meeting up with you to murder you.'

'Why did I agree to this? I feel faint just thinking of his rotten teeth…' Claire shuddered.

'You did not agree to anything,' Mary scoffed. 'This grand scheme was all your design. You are the one who stole the scarf and thought that walking out with him would be a capital idea.'

'Well, now I see it is sheer idiocy,' Claire huffed. 'What were you and Mrs Knapp thinking, to allow me to put such a hare-brained scheme in place?'

'Claire, once you get an idea into your mind, I do not think anyone could stop you, not even Percy.'

'It is nearly time. Talk me through your plan, Mary. Is James coming here?'

'No, James is to meet us at the corner of the road and then we will all walk to Richmond Park. When we reach the entrance, we will stay back and allow you to meet Thomas, but we shall maintain a gentle pace behind you and ensure you are always in our sight.'

'Good, good, I am reassured by that.' Claire nodded. 'Let us go then. I do not want to be late for my gentleman friend.'

Claire clasped Mary's hand tightly, before picking up her scarf and bag and putting on her coat.

Claire's heart pounded as she sat on the bench at the park's entrance. It was quieter today, and she stopped to watch the birds fly from tree to skeletal tree, looking for the last of the year's berries. Their plight was not so different from their own. A gentle tap on her shoulder made Claire turn to see the smiling face of Thomas. His hair was combed and his face scrubbed clean. Even his clothes were tidy. He held his cap in front of him and bowed his head, as if asking her for a dance rather than a stroll. There was something so respectful and traditional in his actions towards her that Claire had to stifle a laugh.

'Hello, Thomas.' She nodded. 'Claire Clairmont.'

'Miss Clairmont,' he replied, holding out his arm.

She hesitated for a heartbeat before accepting it and allowing herself to be swept into the park. Her heart was still racing as they walked past Mary and James, who had positioned themselves on a bench, the low branches of the surrounding tree partially concealing their faces.

'I was worried all morning that you would not show and as I only know you through Mrs Knapp, I thought I would have to go to her house and plead with her tenderest of mercies for your address.'

Claire laughed. 'That would have been no good. She does not know it. We have changed addresses so many times of late that even I struggle to remember it.'

'Really?' Thomas smiled and patted her hand. 'Then we have more in common than I thought.'

\*

Mary bit her lip as she watched Claire walk by. Thomas was almost unrecognisable as the man they'd met before; Claire had clearly made an impression on him and now he was keen to make an impression on her. It would have been sweet if the circumstances had been different, but Mary could not be light or fanciful; she was here to pay attention and ensure that her sister came to no harm. It had surprised her greatly to realise that Claire's wellbeing was so paramount to her; after all, she had spent much of their tour of Paris and Switzerland wishing for Claire's absence by various nefarious means. But when it came down to it, she did not wish her any harm at all.

'He seems attentive,' said James, interrupting her thoughts.

'Yes,' Mary replied. 'He has certainly made an effort to impress.'

'And how is Percy?' James asked. 'Is he well?'

'Yes, wonderful,' Mary replied.

'But he is not with you today?' It was a casual remark, but one that wounded her greatly. Mary sighed. She had waited for Percy at their lodgings the previous night, ignoring her heavy eyelids and tired limbs to hear the church bells chime midnight. In her dreams, she had imagined they would deliver him back to her like a welcome breeze sweeping through the door, blowing out all doubt, hesitation, and loneliness. It had not been so. The bells brought nothing other than a new day, and it was not until almost four hours later that Percy had eventually rolled in, smelling like the barrel he'd been reluctant to leave behind.

'I have seen the baby, Mary!' He could hardly speak through his happy tears. 'Charles is so like myself.'

Mary blinked. If he had seen the baby, that meant he had been in communication with Harriet himself. She crumpled the envelope in her hands — no need for that now Percy had made his own arrangements.

'He has revitalised me, Mary!'

'I believe the alcohol might have something to do with that.' She bit her lip. Of all the ways she had imagined his homecoming, this was not one of them.

'Oh, Mary.' He threw an arm around her, drawing her closer to his acidic breath, which pricked her nostrils. 'Do not be so bitter! You too will have a baby of your own, and perhaps then you will not be so hostile to Harriet's.'

'Hostile to Harriet's!' She thought back to the drenching she'd received from Eliza when trying to sort out Percy's affairs, and her pleading with Harriet to allow him to meet his son. These were not the actions of a jealous and hostile woman, just a woman seeking peace. It was Percy's subterfuge that brought the unnecessary discomfort.

'Let us not fall out. I must be away again soon. I have plans to release some future capital against another short-term loan. Godwin needs…'

'You have heard from my father?' Mary whispered. Thinking of their alienation from her father as being a shared pursuit had somehow made it more acceptable, but to know that Percy was still a welcome part of his life was agony. She swallowed. 'How is Papa? Is he well?'

Percy shrugged. 'He is as he always is, like a bloodhound on the scent of money.'

She rarely allowed herself to think of all she had left behind. *This is the life I chose* had played more frequently in her mind than any sheet ballad. But the casual way in which Percy talked about her father was too much, as if he were nothing more than an inconvenience to be paid off.

'You may do well to remember, dear, that you pursued my father with talk of financial support for his publishing company,' Mary chided. 'In that way, you put yourself in this position that you now scorn. He did not solicit your company, nor prove willing to pay through the nose for it.'

The recollection of the scurrilous rumour that Percy had bought Mary and Claire from Mr Godwin for a thousand pounds made her shudder.

That was enough thinking of Percy for now. Mary blinked and looked at James.

'No, Percy is not with me today,' Mary replied, in answer to his query.


Claire and Thomas had made their way to the island. Without a flaming boat upon it, the water seemed tame and uninteresting. Thomas's talk had been dull and peppered with all he hoped to be, which, in Claire's view, only emphasised how little he had.

'This was where I first saw you…' Thomas stopped, pointing at the clearing between the trees. Claire's heart contracted. Though she did not remember him, she did recall the hands of the man around the woman's throat.

'I have something to show you.' She reached into her bag and pulled out the scarf.

'My necktie!' Thomas exclaimed, eyes wide and hands ready to receive it. Claire held it firm. His expression changed, his brows knitting in confusion. 'That's my work necktie,' he continued. 'I have been looking for it everywhere.' A vein between his eyebrows was suddenly as thick and prominent as a worm. 'Claire, give it back. I ain't joking — they will dock my wages if I lose another one.'

'Who will?' she asked. 'This is not your scarf, Thomas, but one that I found.'

'You found it?' Thomas rubbed his forehead and the vein disappeared as if it had been told to stand down. 'I don't understand — what is going on, Claire? I wanted to walk out with you because I thought you were handsome, but I am getting the strongest of feelings that I am being played for a fool.'

Claire felt a firm grip over her hand, and it took a moment for her to realise it was his.

'I don't like being taken for a fool.' Thomas's eyes were cold now. 'Give me the scarf.'

Claire swallowed and forced a smile. 'I was having a game with you, Thomas. There is no need to be grumpy.' He released the pressure on her hand and she handed him the scarf. Slowly, the anger melted from his expression.

'Forgive me, Claire. It is just that … well, you know I am not a man of independent means and I have many lines of work. I am a butcher's boy in the daytime, and in the evening I run … errands for people.'

'Errands?'

He nodded. 'Sometimes I help people move things. Sometimes it is a message from a tavern to a country house when a man is too inebriated to move his own mouth; this scarf lets people know I'm a runner.'

'You did not buy this scarf?'

'Buy it?' Thomas laughed, his cheeks pink. 'I could not afford to buy a silk scarf on my wages — you have seen my lodgings — and even if I could, it isn't really my colour. I would have to be a right dandy to wear an orange scarf — it wouldn't really match the blood on my apron now, would it?'

Claire breathed out slowly. Money had caused his ill mood; it was nothing more than a spike at the mention of his poverty. His pride had been wounded, that was all. He was no killer, though she wondered at the kinds of jobs he was tasked with in his evening role.

'Will you tell me who gave you this scarf?' she asked innocently.

Thomas shook his head. 'They aren't the sort of people a woman like you should know. I pray to heaven that you don't. I cannot tell you, and you had best forget about it.' He smiled at her. 'Think of it as being a love token given to me by a woman. That will make your heart swell with jealousy, won't it?'

*Not with those teeth*, Claire thought. 'What do you know about your sister's disappearance?'

'Nothing more than I told you the other day. I received word to collect her belongings. That is everything I know.' He shrugged and smiled at her again.


Once Claire had finally shaken Thomas off, she had found Mary and James and together they had returned to their lodgings for tea. James had insisted on buying cakes and treats to accompany the tea, and Mary was grateful that he was providing yet another of her meals. If only Percy felt the same level of responsibility.

'This is all tremendously exciting,' James exclaimed, once Claire had finished telling them about her meeting with Thomas.

'Well, our next step is clear,' Mary added, digging into a cake whose cream sank out of the opposite side as she picked it up. 'We need to follow him in the evening and see where he goes.'

Claire shook her head. 'I think he will expect that. He knows that there is more to the business with the scarf than I was letting on; it was obvious in my reluctance to return the scarf to him and in his eagerness to get it back. We cannot possibly follow him as we are.'

'So what do we do instead?' James leant forward.

'I can hardly go chasing around the London streets in my condition.' Mary sighed. 'I am exhausted after one of our walks.' She shook her head. 'No. You two must do it. Or you must wait until Percy has returned and then he can go with you.'

'We cannot wait!' Claire shrilled. 'Time is of the essence, and we have lost enough of it as it is. I have an idea and I think it is highly effective.'

Mary groaned inwardly. 'And just what is your tremendous idea?'

'We had one scarf, then for a moment we had two scarves…' Claire's eyes widened.

'And?' Mary tried to hurry her along.

'What if we had two scarves again and were able to follow Thomas around whilst wearing them?'

'You mean pretend that we are errand boys like him?' James asked.

'Yes, precisely that. It cannot be so difficult to make another scarf like this. Any milliners would have fabric enough for us to make our own.'

'You are forgetting, Claire, that we have absolutely no money. We scarcely have enough food to eat, let alone money to squander on neckties.'

Mary caught James's eye; her cheeks flamed at the sympathy she detected there.

'That is easily remedied; I shall buy the necktie,' he said. 'Mary, you can come with me to buy it if you like?'

Mary noticed Claire's face fall.

'Thank you, James. I will buy the necktie and Claire shall be the errand boy. I cannot possibly run all the way around London, as you know.' Mary looked at Claire. A smile had returned to her lips.

# CHAPTER EIGHT

'Are you sure you want to do this, Claire?'

'I feel perfectly safe, Mary.' Claire tied the necktie around her neck. Mary tutted and corrected it. 'Besides, it is not like I will be alone. James will be there and he is such a calming presence, is he not? But with eminent authority.'

Mary nodded her silent agreement. She would love nothing more than to race along the London streets following Thomas, but the risk of harm to the baby was too great and so she reluctantly agreed to stay at home. Her reverie was disturbed by a knock at the door. Mary opened it to reveal James Berry, decked out in the same work clothes and necktie as Claire. From a distance, they could be mistaken for working men, and the shade of night doused everything with the haze of uncertainty.

Her eyes widened when she saw his orange necktie. 'You found the scarf!'

'I did. It caused some consternation and entertainment for the gentlemen in the tailors when I gave the specific details of the colour and silk. It is a style from several seasons hence,' he explained.

'I think we look splendid.' Claire slapped him on the shoulder and they stood together; a more dubious set of errand boys London had never seen. 'Let us go.'

Claire couldn't help but feel that something would go wrong. Despite her earlier protestations to Mary and her best attempts to seem sure of the success of their plan, doubts crept in. She wished it were Percy by her side rather than this new friend of

Mary's, who was no substitute for Percy at all. As they walked to Thomas Bell's lodgings, her senses were sharpened by the harsh smell of lime and marshes that coated the air. All the people they passed were stooped and curved, bent double by their brutal circumstances and impossible living conditions; there was no wealth here, nor was it to be found in the neighbourhood. They would cut through London, weaving a path through the mean streets that led to the dark places brightened by ill deeds in velvet rooms. What they would find when they got there would be the gateway to the crime she had witnessed and would hopefully enable them to bring the matter to a close.

Thomas appeared hours into their watch. Claire might not have noticed had James not nudged her back to wakefulness. A neighbourhood cat was disturbed and let out a shriek which warned of Thomas's presence. His dress mirrored their own, but was dirty and worn, and he carried an oil lamp in his hand, which he swung with a whistle as he walked. How different it was to be a man, Claire thought. How much easier to go about a life without constraint or fear; even their clothes were easier to move in. James gestured for them to follow at a distance and the night provided many hiding places for them to quickly jump into whenever Thomas's ears were pricked by their movement.

They followed him through the markets, which night had cast in an entirely different hue. The flower stalls had a putrid note that matched the discarded meats and fish. Thomas spoke to a man who had cast aside the decorative adornments of polite society; his shirt had become loose and his shirt sleeves were rolled up to the elbows. Neither Claire nor James could hear the subject of their conversation, but as coins glistened in the moonlight, the nature of their transaction was clear.

Something the man said made Thomas nod and look around him before whistling and disappearing out of sight. Claire went to follow, but James held her back and shook his head.

'No,' he said firmly. 'Let us give them a minute to disband, then we may follow where he leads.'

Claire nodded her agreement. Sure enough, the man followed in the direction Thomas had taken, past the market stalls, towards the shops on Savile Row and then behind them. Something ran across Claire's foot and as she caught sight of its long, pink tail, she put a hand to her mouth before her scream could give them away.

'There are lots of rats around here,' James whispered. 'It is all the debris from the market.'

Claire swallowed down the nausea that clogged her throat. If the smell of rotten earth was bad, it was nothing compared to the smell of decaying animal flesh; it clung to her nostrils, and she doubted whether it would ever leave again.

'Where are they going?'

'It looks as though they are going behind the shops,' James replied. 'Come on.'

They abandoned their hiding place, making use of the dark shadows from stalls and buildings to mask their advancement. Behind the shops there was a different texture to the ground, and the cobbles slowed Claire down until she became accustomed to them. The tidy façades and displays of the shops would do little to persuade a customer to make a purchase if they saw the disarray of their rears, Claire thought; boxes and wrappers merged with mud and dirt, providing palatial homes for rodent nests. Claire made a mental note to stay as far away from their kingdom as possible. Fortunately, Thomas and his friend did not stop here; they moved further still to a row of sheds and containers behind the shops.

'Those must be the workshops,' James mused.

Just then, the sound of horses' hooves on the cobblestones broke the silence, though Claire could see no sign of the horses that made them. 'Perhaps there is a track behind the workshops?' she suggested.

'There is only one way to find out.' James dashed forward. Claire ducked down and followed him. James wove a path through the darkness until he found a sheltered position. Thomas came into view, closing the packaging of a crate. Once the crate was closed, he was joined by the other man, who had taken off his jacket and was now helping Thomas to move the crate onto a wheeled truck. Quiet words and laughter accompanied their actions, Thomas wiping sweat off his forehead with a dirty sleeve that left a dark mark that even the night could not hide.

'Whatever they are doing, it is heavy work for the two of them,' Claire said through clenched teeth.

'Down!' James suddenly hissed, pushing her to the floor.

Thomas appeared in front of them, holding his oil lamp up in the air. He looked around and then shook his head. Claire's heart beat loudly in her ears as he disappeared again, whistling once more. They stayed low on the ground until the coast was clear.

A light scratching sound reminded Claire that they had encroached on vermin territory. She swallowed and turned back to the task at hand. As Thomas wheeled the crate, his lamp threw flickers of light onto the scene and she saw a darkened store; there was a bench with tools on top and an unlit lamp.

'What do you imagine that is?' she whispered.

James shook his head. 'I do not know. It looks to be a work shed, perhaps? It must belong to the business.'

They watched as Thomas and the other man took a path to the right, in the opposite direction from where they had come. Claire and James followed at a distance. A sharp whistle was heard, and Thomas wheeled the crate in that direction.

'Is that a post chaise?' Claire asked, squinting into the darkness.

A driver had stepped down from the carriage and was helping them to secure the crate onto the chaise. The horses neighed their disapproval of the weight of the new load. Thomas and the other man exchanged words before Thomas blew out his lamp and got into the carriage. A light tap on the carriage roof seemed to be the conclusion of their business, and the other man stepped back as the driver climbed back into position and drove off. Fearing they may be seen, Claire pushed James back into a nook; they were so close together that she could see the flash of uncertainty that crossed his brow. Perhaps he had never been in this situation before. His jaw was clenched tight and he was hardly breathing. Once the man's heeled shoes had faded away on the cobbles, Claire peeled herself away from James.

'I think we have lost him,' she said.

'Yes.' James nodded and took a deep breath. 'What a tremendously exciting evening this has been.'

Claire wondered if he was only talking about their investigation.

'What do we do now?' he asked.

'Now we go back and tell Mary everything we have learned so she may help us make sense of it all.'

Mary threw the book aside. She had tried to immerse herself in Greek verbs, then philosophy, then travel, but her mind would not stray further than the Lambeth marshes and her nerves were tight with anticipation and apprehension. It was some consolation to know that James was with Claire, but her own heart felt the silence of Percy's absence like the cold draught that had crept into every vacant part of the lodging.

As the hours dragged by, fatigue had held her hostage, weighing down her body, even though her mind was sharp and active. Mary focused on the rhythmic ticking of the clock, but it was no good — tiredness forced her to close her eyes for a few hours.

Sometime after midnight, muffled voices on the stairs heralded the arrival of Claire and James, and Mary swept to the door to hush them before they woke up the landlady and the rest of the house. The boy with the kettle drum upstairs needed no nocturnal invitation to party.

'Get in here quickly,' she mouthed.

James and Claire dived into the room, Claire immediately discarding her cap and scarf, throwing them to the floor. It had not taken her long to assume masculine habits as well as masculine attire.

'I hope you are not going to leave that there, Claire.'

The reminder of her name broke the spell and Claire picked up the items and placed them neatly on the table.

'Sorry, Mary,' she replied, rubbing her eyes before untying her boots.

'Thank you, Claire, for a capital evening.' James bowed. It was as if they had been to the theatre rather than on the scent of murder. 'I shall take my leave of you both now. Mary, the public lecture I told you of is on Friday, if you wish to accompany me?'

'Thank you, James. That would be wonderful.'

'Very well, until Friday then. Goodnight.' He bowed again and left the room. Mary closed the door quietly behind him and turned back to Claire.

'We have walked all over London,' said Claire, yawning. 'I will need to bathe my feet in the morning, but I fear you will not get much sense out of me this evening, Mary. I need to rest now.'

Mary slumped into the chair, huffing. All that waiting around and putting off her own sleep was not to be rewarded with even the slightest crumb of information from either of them? She had sharpened her quill, ready to make notes. Indignation battled fatigue for dominance, and Mary allowed the dizzying sensation that had taken hold to transform itself into sleep. Soon her body was so heavy she doubted she would be able to drag it from the chair to her bed; she certainly harboured no illusions that she would have time or mind enough to change into her nightdress. The sisters rolled into their beds and grunted goodnight to each other before closing their eyes to the world.

The monster who haunted her dreams was waiting for her behind her eyelids. Mary was a child again, standing at the edge of the sea, watching as the crashing waves gushed up in foamy pockets that covered her feet before dissolving away again. The monster was next to her, his bone-white fingers so close that they brushed her elbow. When he turned to face her, he had taken on the dishevelled hair of Thomas Bell and the dark, sunken eyes of the hungry people they had become. It brought a sense of relief to know that this monster was nothing more than a patchwork of her thoughts. *I can control you*, she thought. *The blood that flows through my veins brings you to life and you will bend to my will*. Suddenly the world around her shook, the land collapsing into the sea, trees folding in on one another like a funeral pyre. She was no longer a child. She was full of the secrets of life. Mary watched herself, stretched out on the water like a star; the gentle undulations of the waves felt like a soft hand rocking her.

'Mary! Mary, wake up. James Berry is here!'

Mary rubbed her eyes and sat up. Claire's tousled hair and dishevelled clothing indicated that she too had fallen asleep in her clothes rather than her night attire.

'You are going to have to see to him while I get changed. At least you are dressed.'

Mary looked down at her crumpled dress and sighed. 'Very well,' she said. 'I will take him out for a brief walk around the park; you must get yourself and this place fit for visitors.'

Claire nodded, scrambling to gather her clothes.

'And open the window,' Mary added. 'It smells musty.' She opened the door to their guest. 'James!' she greeted. 'What a pleasant surprise. We were not expecting to see you again until Friday.'

'I know, but I bring breakfast gifts…' He held out a package. 'I was hoping that we might digest the results of last night's expedition whilst chewing on these.' He tittered, clearly amused by his own joke.

'Let us put these in the room and take a quick stroll. I always find a walk prepares the body well for breaking fast, don't you?'

'Most heartily.' He laughed again. If he was going to carry on in this excited vein, then it would become irritating very quickly. Mary longed to return to bed, weary after her broken sleep.

She had not looked at the clock and imagined, purely from the tiredness that fogged her thoughts, that the hour was early;

but the winter sky was well established and the roads busy with the hustle and bustle of mid-morning.

'I have lectures this afternoon, but I could not wait to hear your opinions on last night's events.'

Mary frowned. 'I would love to be able to share my opinions, but given that Claire has not yet divulged any of the events of last night, I am unable to do so.' She sighed. 'She was too tired to do anything but sleep.'

'I suppose we did walk a long way,' James said, 'but it was worth it.'

'Perhaps you will summarise all that happened and then we can discuss it over tea and a pastry. I suppose the most important question is, did you follow Thomas Bell?'

'Yes, we did. We managed to follow him until he got into a carriage. He went to the markets, where he met a man.'

'What sort of man?'

'A man of some standing, I would say; perhaps a businessman. Some sort of payment was made.'

'What happened then?'

'They disappeared into a workshop behind the shops on Savile Row. Thomas wheeled out a wooden crate.'

'A crate?' Mary asked.

James nodded enthusiastically. 'Yes, a crate, like a shipping crate.'

'Or one used to smuggle…' Mary trailed off and tapped her lip with her finger. 'We know that Thomas has very little money — is it a stretch to imagine that where money is concerned, he has little morality?'

'You think he was involved in some criminal enterprise?' James gasped, his eyes wide with excitement.

'Perhaps. I do not think he is the mastermind behind it — he does not have the means, nor the capacity — but perhaps he might *assist* in it? An ask-no-questions-so-long-as-he-is-paid kind of assistance.'

'I would not wish to generalise,' James spluttered.

Mary shook her head. 'No, neither would I. But I do not think it is unreasonable to suppose that an empty stomach might make a man sink to lows he had not thought himself capable of.' She did not mention that she herself had recently been tempted to steal a piece of fruit from a market stall out of sheer hunger.

'I suppose you could be right.' James shrugged. 'Who knows what people are capable of?'

'What happened next?' Mary asked. The talk of empty stomachs had made her own start to rumble.

'Nothing. They took the package to a waiting carriage and drove off.'

'They could have been taking it to the docks for transportation,' Mary mused, piecing the puzzle together in her mind. 'But where were they going?'

'I suppose a great many items are transported by water overnight,' James added. 'The sea would be quieter without the package steamers.'

Mary's mind was transported back to the summer, when her life had been an endless cycle of carriages, steamers, and boats. For a moment she could smell the salty water, the fish heads and the vomit of the drunken men. She breathed deeply to remind her senses that they were not there. London had its own sights and smells, but at least they were mostly hidden in the daytime, thank goodness. The air today was fresh with a gentle winter's bite — infinitely preferable.

'Perhaps it is simply my overactive imagination concluding that a crime has taken place.' Mary shrugged. 'There may be a perfectly reasonable explanation. It could be nothing more than Thomas needing the money provided by working day and night.'

'Perhaps. But that still does not tell us why he went to Mrs Knapp's house claiming to be Annie's brother.'

Mary paused to gather her thoughts and consider their next steps. 'We need to go back to the shops on Savile Row and the workrooms behind them, to see if we can find the man you saw with Thomas last night. We also need to find out if Thomas has a sister and if he does, if she is Mrs Knapp's missing servant.'

# CHAPTER NINE

'It is good to see you again, Mary. I was wondering how you were getting on with your investigations.' Mrs Knapp sniffed as she uttered the word *investigations*, as if it was a disease that could be caught.

Mrs Knapp showed Mary into the kitchen and ushered her into one of the skeletal chairs.

'I've come with a few questions about Annie Bell.'

'Ask away, dear. I don't suppose there's much I can tell you, though.'

'Was she like Thomas in appearance? Was there any similarity between them?'

Mrs Knapp frowned in concentration. 'When he came here claiming to be her brother and collected her things, he was alone. I never saw them together. It is easier to see the similarity between things when they're placed side by side.'

Mary nodded and waited.

'Annie has the same dark hair as Thomas, but there was none of the harshness. He looks like what he is — a young lad trying to make a living in these mean streets. She didn't have that quality; she was not worldly enough for London.'

'What do you mean, not worldly?'

'She told me she'd escaped from a bad family, but she was innocent to the ways of the world and not ready for it.'

'She never mentioned a brother?'

Mrs Knapp shook her head. 'Not to me.'

'How long was Annie with you?'

'Three months or thereabouts. Not long.'

Mary sighed. 'I cannot shake the feeling that Annie may have been the woman Claire saw in the park, but with no body, there is no way of knowing.' She slumped down in the chair. This case seemed to be one step forward and two giant leaps backward. It was only to give Claire peace of mind that she had even taken it on; she had worries enough of her own without adding to her burden. There was a perpetual ache in her heart since Percy had left, which nothing but his company would remedy. Notes and letters from him had been few, and when they were delivered by the errand boys, they were short and to the point: *Going to see the lawyers* or *All this will be sorted soon*. There was none of his former tenderness, no poetry, no affection. Her scarf was a poor substitute for the weight of his arm around her, shielding her with his warmth.

'When is the baby due?' Mrs Knapp asked, smiling and nodding towards Mary's stomach.

'Spring.' Mary sat back and rubbed her stomach, which fluttered in response. There. There was her connection to Percy. How could she ever feel alone?

'What does Mr Godwin have to say on the matter?' Mrs Knapp shuffled in her seat.

'He has not spoken to me directly since I left for France with Percy.' Mary swallowed. 'I am not welcome at the house, and no one comes to visit me. I suppose he is ashamed of me.' Her heart sank with the sadness she had become accustomed to.

'He is a fool.' Mrs Knapp folded her arms. 'It is all that Mary Jane's influence. I never met a woman more spiteful. It makes her day to hurt someone else.' Mrs Knapp shook her head.

It made Mary smile to hear another articulate her most secret thoughts. Having Claire as her constant companion made it impossible for Mary to talk about her feelings on the matter, but her father *had* changed since his marriage to Mary Jane, and not for the better.

'Anyway,' said Mrs Knapp, 'that's enough talk about her. Make yourself comfortable while I make us something to eat, and then we can discuss this mystery of yours.'

The mystery remained unsolved, but at least Mary's stomach was satiated, and the baby kicked with satisfaction as she made her way back to their lodgings. As she opened the door, Claire rushed towards her, blocking her view of the room.

'Mary, you are back! We have a visitor.' Claire's eyes sparkled. Mary's own eyes narrowed. Something was afoot. Claire didn't usually greet her with such excitement. What was the cause of it? Surely, she had not allowed Thomas Bell to know where they lived? It would be a grave mistake if she had.

'Claire, I hope you have not forgotten that our landlady does not allow gentlemen callers unless they are doctors.' Technically, this made James Berry's visits to them perfectly acceptable. 'Let me in.'

Claire tittered before finally opening the door to reveal the best surprise that Mary could have wished for.

Percy. Right there, in the flesh, with all his curls and alabaster skin.

'Percy!' Mary cried before rushing into his arms, allowing herself to be whirled around. The strength of his arms around her made the tension of the previous weeks melt away. Her entire body relaxed, and she closed her eyes in a dizzying ecstasy of relief. Soon, grateful tears fell from her eyes and dampened his shoulder.

'Why are you crying, Mary? Are you not pleased to see me?' he teased.

'You know that these are tears of joy and relief.' She smacked his shoulder, reluctantly stepping back from his arms. 'Oh, Percy, please tell me this is a permanent return?'

'It is, my love. I have valiantly fought the creditors and my grandfather, and he has agreed to increase my stipend and has given me a thousand pounds. I think he has given it to me to be rid of me.'

'Well, his wanting to be rid of you has brought you back to me, and for that I am eternally in his debt.' Mary pressed her lips to his, closing her eyes so she could savour the kiss. His lips were petal-soft, and her thoughts dropped away as she kissed them. 'You must tell me everything you have been up to, where you have been, what you have read, what you have written.' She led him over to the sofa.

'I am afraid there is little to report on any of those fronts, Mary. Being absent from my muse has robbed me of the power to enjoy life; there have been no books or poetry, no talk of philosophy, just a daily grind of running from place to place like the fox trying to outrun the hounds. They were baying for my blood, but I have tricked them at every turn!' Percy's eyes flashed with familiar pride.

'But here, there have been significant changes, so Claire has been telling me. I believe she has become a nightwatchman.' Percy laughed. Claire shook her head and looked at him; they too had fallen back into their easy camaraderie. This was their arrangement at its best, nothing but love and friendship.

'I will have you know I would make a good watchman or Bow Street Runner,' Claire replied. 'I have a great nose for trouble and an instinct for justice.'

'Tell me everything about the case; have you solved it yet?' Percy put his arms around Claire and Mary. 'Oh, it is good to be back with my two favourite women!'

Mary smiled, but there was something about his hand resting on Claire's shoulder that ignited a flicker of jealousy. Claire turned her face to Percy's and placed her hand on his knee. Mary breathed deeply, not daring to observe Percy's reaction. When Claire patted it lightly, Mary breathed a sigh of relief.

'I will make tea. Mary has been out at Mrs Knapp's this morning. I'm sure there is much to tell you.'

Was it her imagination, or did James Berry seem a little put out when Percy joined them on their mission to retrace the steps of their nocturnal pursuit? He had been politeness itself, holding out his hand to Percy and accepting the handshake with firm grace, but there had been something in his slight smile that spoke of disappointment. Mary shook the thoughts away; trying to second-guess the feelings of others was never a worthy endeavour.

There was no disguising Percy's feelings. He was well and truly saddened that he had missed so much of the investigation. That his shoes had been filled by James Berry was perhaps the reason why Percy chose to take charge at the head of the walk, as if he were leading them into battle. The fact that he had to be directed several times by Claire and James revealed the superficiality of his authority and eventually he slunk back, keeping pace with Mary, who had to keep stopping to rub her back. She could have sworn that her stomach had doubled in size in the day since Percy had returned.

When they finally reached the shops, everyone agreed the journey had taken its toll on them and Percy slipped into a nearby tavern, smuggling out tankards of ale, which helped to revive them. Mary sipped at the top of Percy's, drinking just enough to give herself a renewed sense of vigour and to leave a bitter aftertaste of yeast in her mouth.

Claire frowned as they passed the cobbles. 'It all looked very different at night. It could have been anywhere.' She shrugged.

James pointed towards an alcove hidden between two shops.

'This is definitely where Thomas met that man. It must have been one of these shops.'

'Which one?' Mary asked.

James shook his head. 'Of that I am not sure. A door opened, a man came out and then they made their way behind the shops.'

'Let us go back there.' Percy clapped. 'Perhaps that will jog your memory, Claire?'

Without the sheen of moonlight and with the addition of scores of men moving boxes, carting things around and filling the air with obscenities when something went wrong or someone got in the way, Mary feared Claire would not remember anything. Her fears were unfounded.

'Look, there!' Claire suddenly cried. 'That was it; I recognise the tools.'

'There?' Percy laughed disdainfully. 'That's nothing but a cobbler's workshop!'

True enough, there were shoes on the workbench.

'You are sure that's where you saw them?' Percy scratched his head. 'I cannot imagine there is much trade to be done with shoes?'

Mary could not help but agree, but curiosity made her move closer towards it. 'A cobbler's workshop it might be, but is it customary for it to have sawdust on the floor?'

*

'Just so I am clear on everything,' Percy said later, when he, Mary and Claire were back at their lodgings, 'Thomas Bell may or may not have something to do with what Claire saw in the park, but we don't think he is the murderer; the victim may or may not be Mrs Knapp's missing help, Annie; and there's a group of errand boys going around London town wearing the same orange neckties, presumably to identify them as belonging to this group? Have I missed anything?'

Mary rubbed her temples. 'No, that sums it up. But when you put it like that, it seems like the work of a fanciful afternoon, not almost a month.'

Percy shrugged. 'The Paris investigation took almost two.'

'You would think that a murder committed in front of someone in a public place would be easier to solve, but no.' Mary bit her lip.

'I am back now — perhaps together we will find the clues that have so far evaded you.'

Mary bit down on the temptation to reply to that. Instead she said, 'We need to find out more about this group that Thomas is in, but how?'

'A trip around the taverns and coffee houses might provide us with that.'

'Coffee houses?' cried Claire. 'Women cannot be seen in coffee houses. Our reputations will be ruined.'

Mary's brow creased. The question of reputation was one that had caused her much heartache and many sleepless nights over the past six months. '*Your* reputation remains intact, Claire. I am the fallen woman without hope.' Mary's voice was flat. 'Can you fetch me some paper, please? We must add to our notes.'

Claire pouted but did as she was asked.

'James is not joining us to add his *opinions*?' asked Percy lightly, though the last word held more than a hint of disdain. He was clearly stung by the fact that in his absence James had occupied the position of the male of the household — if only on a friendly, casual basis.

'He has lectures this afternoon,' Mary explained.

'The eminent doctor.' Percy sniffed. 'I thought about becoming a doctor, but I reasoned that I would better serve the world with philanthropy and philosophy.'

'Do not forget poetry,' Mary said with a smile.

'I have not forgotten,' Percy replied and a fire ignited behind his eyes, a fire that confirmed all traces of his former melancholy had been extinguished.

'Right.' Mary snapped them back to action, picking up the quill. 'I have added notes to what is known; now we must list what is left to do.'

'We need to investigate Thomas Bell's gang,' Percy chimed in.

'And we need to find out more about Annie, assuming she is the woman I saw in the park,' said Claire.

'Even if she is not, she is the only lead we have — unless we are to go to every household and business in London to find out if there is another missing woman.'

'Well,' said Percy, 'we should consider what type of woman would be in the park with a man at night; it will not be your governess or teacher, will it?'

Mary gave Percy an incredulous look. 'Women, like men, should be free to come and go as they please, to follow any path they wish to take — except criminality, of course.'

'I am merely saying what society dictates…' Percy tried to backtrack but trailed off, aware of the hopelessness of the endeavour.

'He has a point.' Claire turned to Mary. 'Mr Godwin would never allow you to go out with Percy alone unless I was there as chaperone. It isn't done. To be meeting up in the park does rather suggest that the couple had nowhere else to go.'

'Do you think he was married?' Mary asked.

'The marital status of the man is neither here nor there,' Percy replied. 'A man can woo wherever he has a mind to, but meeting a woman in a park at night either tells of a need for secrecy or of a man who has to keep moving.' His cheeks flushed. Of course, he would know all about this. 'A man with debts is a hounded man.' Percy shook his head. The clouds may have lifted, but the sky was not yet entirely clear.

'Finding out more about the necktie gang is a good idea.' Claire folded her hands on her knees. 'Now that we have Percy and James, we have a little gang of our own.'

'That's it!' Mary jumped up from her seat. The baby twisted in disapproval of the sudden movement. 'That is exactly what we need to do! Once we have uncovered more about them, Percy and James need to join!'

Percy huffed. 'Join a gang? I have never been in a gang in my life. I avoided all forms of sport at Eton and staunchly refused to fag.'

Mary ignored him, turning her attention back to Claire. 'Do we know where James got his necktie from?' When Claire shook her head, she said, 'We must ask again when we see him.'

'Have we planned to see him?' Percy asked. 'He seems to have made himself most valuable to you in my absence, Mary.' He pursed his lips. Was that jealousy? It was as near to jealousy as Percy was likely to get.

'Percy,' she replied, 'you know he came to my aid when I had walked to Eliza's house on *your behalf*.' She emphasised the last words, reminding him that all of her actions had been for his benefit alone. 'Do you not consider that my intervention helped to soften Harriet's feelings towards you and enabled you to meet your son?'

Percy shrugged. 'I think it might also have something to do with the fact her father tried to *shoot* me.'

Mary gave a dismissive wave. 'Whatever you think, James has been a good friend to us and a most helpful assistant in this matter. I have no romantic inclinations towards him, if that is what you fear, and he has none towards me. Am I keen to make a match between him and Claire? Possibly.' Mary looked at Claire, whose expression was halfway between shock and disgust.

'I would rather walk out with Thomas Bell than James Berry.' She folded her arms. 'There is a flatness to James's personality; at least Thomas has some spark.'

Mary smirked. 'I knew you liked him, despite his teeth.'

Claire shook her head. 'I have heard rumours that Lord Byron is in London for the winter months; he has been seen at a play. If I am to tip my cap in any direction, it will be his.' She inhaled sharply as a thought struck her. 'Do you think he might be at the Royal College of Surgeons this evening?' Her eyes widened hopefully. 'I must change!' Claire scurried around, picking up items of clothing before retiring to the other room.

Mary and Percy exchanged a knowing look before a sudden awkwardness descended upon them, like an unexpected mist on a clear day. Mary brushed out the feathers of the quill; Percy looked out of the window.

'I had forgotten how the light streams through the window.' He shifted in his seat.

'Yes,' Mary replied, straightening herself up.

It was strange that she had wished so much for his return and yet their former easiness was quickly snatched away. There had been no time for them to be alone since he had returned, their thoughts and actions dominated by their desire to solve the murder. Her entire body had trembled with relief when he had returned, as if a lost part had been returned and made her complete. She knew he felt the same way about her, but still there was this awkwardness, as if they were strangers trying to make polite conversation about the weather or the key points and players of a season. Part of her wanted to be swept up in his arms so they could communicate in the most effective language they had — the language of their bodies; but there was no time or space for that and though Claire had left the room, her excited chatter could still be heard, highlighting the stiff silence between them.

'What do you think?' Claire spun into the room, clad in her best frock, her hair piled high on top of her head in a parody of the Parisian fashion. 'Is it too much?' As Claire spun around, the black velvet ribbons on the dress caught the light like a magpie's iridescent tail feathers. They stood out against the blood-red skirt of the gown.

'I have not seen you in that dress before,' said Mary.

'No, you have not. It is from Mama. She purchased it but thought the red too bold for a lady of her years.' Claire twirled around again, stopping at Percy. 'What do you think of it, Percy?'

'I think it is capital,' he replied, nodding. 'It is very bold, as you say, but most fitting for an evening on medical matters.'

'I shall temper it with my black cloak.' Claire was talking to herself now, even though she was nodding at Percy. 'Perhaps I will fix my hair back into a bun. You do not think that would be too plain, Mary?'

Mary looked down at her own dress. It was chestnut-brown faded to the colour of winter wood; the small daisies that dotted the bodice now looked like formless splotches.

'No, Claire. I think it would be perfect.'

# CHAPTER TEN

'Are you sure we've come to the right place?' Claire pulled her shawl around her shoulders as they stood outside the Royal College of Surgeons. There was barely enough light to cast shadows; even the streetlamps seemed to quiver.

'James is over there, so we must be. James!' Mary called out. Several heads turned, except for the one she was hoping for. 'He must not have heard me.' She turned to Percy. 'I'll go over and let him know we are here.'

'You do that,' Percy replied swiftly. Mary looked to see if any sign of jealousy marked his face. Finding it devoid of anything except blank curiosity, she made her way over to James.

'Excuse me.' She pushed her way through the crowd, apologising as she went, the smell of sweat filling the air. There was nothing like a free event to bring out the crowds — public executions or dissections; it was all the same to the braying crowds who treated it all like a holiday lark. She could see them glugging gin and moonshine from brown bottles, laughing toothlessly at some half-heard joke. The sound of shattering glass made her jump and Mary closed her eyes; someone in the crowd cheered, and when she opened her eyes again, James was standing in front of her.

'Thank goodness!' Mary cried. 'I thought I'd never reach you.'

'Indeed,' said James, 'it is very busy this evening. I haven't seen crowds like this since Humphry Davy's final lecture at the Royal Institution.'

'You were there?' Mary's eyes widened. 'I was there too.'

The memory fizzed like a sudden current, jolting her back to happier, easier times when she'd attended lectures at the Royal Institution with her father; then the spark was extinguished by the thought of their present-day relationship. She sighed. There was no hope of resuscitating that relationship, not while she stayed with Percy, but with his baby growing inside her, there was nowhere else for her to go, no one for her to go to. She looked at James, wondering — just for the briefest of moments — if he could bring up another man's child. He caught her staring at him and frowned.

'What is it, Mary?'

'Sorry.' She shook the notion out of her mind and breathed deeply. 'Thinking of Davy just brought my father to mind. I was struck by a sudden melancholy, but it has passed now.'

James held out his arm, and Mary linked hers through it. 'I am most pleased to hear it. A woman like you should only have happy thoughts.'

She forced a weak smile and hoped that it was enough to conceal the genuine emotions that swam beneath it.

'I believe a dissection is on the menu for this evening.' James laughed. 'Do you have the appetite for it?'

'What an unfortunate choice of metaphor, James.' They walked in synchronised steps. 'I have no problem with blood and guts, but I hope you have smelling salts on hand for others of our party whose stomachs are more sensitive than my own.'

'Claire?'

Mary shook her head. 'No, Percy.' She lowered her head as she whispered, 'He says it is the only reason he could not pursue a medical career; I think there may have been others.'

They continued on until they reached Percy and Claire. Percy was watching the crowd with open-mouthed amazement;

Claire had turned her back on the crowd and had made Percy her sole focus.

'I have never seen so many drunken people in one place.' She sniffed the air, then tutted, shaking her head as she did so.

'It is almost Christmas, Claire,' Percy replied. 'People are looking for amusement to light up these long nights.'

Claire huffed. 'I prefer to spend my nights reading books and broadening my mind.'

'Shall I walk you back then?' Percy asked. 'If the crowd is upsetting you too much? Only…' Percy hesitated. 'I thought I saw Byron in the crowd over there.'

'He is here?' Claire spun around. 'Lord Byron, the poet?'

'I would hardly tell you about the whereabouts of George Byron the Butcher on Long Acre now, would I?'

'Byron is here? You have seen him?' Claire clutched at her heaving chest. Mary stifled a giggle. What a rotter Percy could be. Thomas Bell was more likely to be here than Byron, who was probably at a fine ball in Almack's Assembly Rooms or in a box at the opera. What appeal would dissection have to a man of poetry and philosophy — a man who believed in the ethereal and the unexplained, not the rational and proven? Still, if he was here, he could not fail to miss Claire's exotic outfit and elaborate hairstyle.

The heavy green doors opened, casting a welcome light onto the crowd, who cheered as they swelled forward, eager to position themselves in the best spots with the clearest view of the body.

'Do we know what the subject of the lecture will be?' asked Mary.

'The physiognomy of the human heart,' James answered.

Mary laughed. 'It is a question that has baffled scientists and poets alike throughout the centuries. I fear we may be here all night.'

The four made their way towards the entrance. Mary hadn't noticed the point at which James had removed his arm from hers, allowing Percy to slide his through hers instead, but it felt ceremonial; being with Percy always felt like being in the right place, her natural place.

'Mary, look!' Claire was standing on tiptoes, peering over the heads in the crowd. 'I think I see him. There, look, is that not his hair?'

Mary presumed Claire was talking about Byron, but knew there was no way she could distinguish his head from a sea of others.

'Claire, I would have difficulty picking myself out from this crowd, let alone someone whose likeness I have scarcely seen.'

'It is him; I am sure of it.' Claire squeezed Mary's hand excitedly.

They were herded into the room. 'Over here,' James said, tilting his head towards a staircase. 'We can watch from the gallery. There are seats there.'

'It will be like having our own private box.' Claire smiled. 'And it will provide a most thorough view of everyone below. Lead the way.'

James took them up the stairway and into the gallery in which a couple of men were already seated. They stood up, coughed and nodded greetings towards the party. Claire and Mary took two seats in the front row whilst Percy was left to hesitantly take a seat next to James. Below, two finely dressed men walked out and bowed to the crowd, as if about to take to the stage and start singing. They walked with the confidence of men of status, aware that their knowledge of the issues about to be described exceeded that of the crowd. Both were in middle to upper age, but whereas one was shorter with small eyes magnified by thick, rimless spectacles, the other was straight-backed, with a thick mane of greying hair streaked like a badger's. It was he who spoke first.

'Good evening, ladies and gentlemen. I am Dr Harper and this is my colleague Dr Hume, and this evening we are going to reveal to you the secrets of the human heart.'

'He may well be working on mine if I glimpse Byron,' Claire whispered. Mary hushed her, keen not to miss anything. She listened as the two men continued talking, but Mary could not resist a glance around the gathered audience below them. Though she lacked Claire's desperation to meet Byron in the flesh, it certainly would be thrilling to share space with the author of *Childe Harold's Pilgrimage*. The men parted, revealing the surgeon's table behind them, covered with a stark white sheet. As they moved, their feet dislodged specks of sawdust that floated into the air. Dr Hume pulled the sheet away from the table like a mesmerist performing a trick, and the audience gasped at the sight of a waxy, naked body on the table.

'Is that an actual body?' Claire turned to ask James.

Her question travelled downwards, and the eyes of the audience were momentarily diverted from the table and cast upwards to her instead.

'Yes, this is a human body,' Dr Harper replied, before swiftly moving towards the head.

'The heart is the most important organ in the human body. We cannot live without it. Once the heart stops, we stop.' Dr Harper picked up a scalpel that glinted in the half-light, and drew a line with the blade across the skin of the chest, leaving a long trail of blood.

Claire put her hand over her eyes and threw herself onto Mary's shoulder. 'Oh!' she exclaimed.

Mary sat forward, transfixed by the unveiling of the human body, as it if were nothing more than an envelope being sliced open. Soon the chest cavity was exposed, pinned open like ruby butterfly wings. Thuds from the floor below confirmed it was not a simple thing to behold, and though Mary felt a little queasy, the feeling was equalled by the strength of her curiosity and she determined to keep her eyes trained on the scene. She breathed deeply just as a ribcage was snapped like a twig.

'Oh, this is too much,' Claire groaned beside her. 'It is making me feel sick.'

Mary swallowed. 'Really, Claire, this is quite fascinating. I have never seen a human dissection before.'

'You will see another dead body if I do not get some air. I must get out of here.'

Mary turned to look at Percy and James. James — like her — was engrossed in the spectacle playing out before them, while Percy's face looked a little ashen.

'Percy,' Mary whispered, 'can you take Claire outside? She is feeling unwell.'

'Very well,' he grumbled, rolling his eyes as if it were too much of an ordeal for him to contemplate. Mary saw through these theatrics, knowing he was secretly glad of the chance to be out of there.

'Come on, Claire,' Percy chided. 'Let us make our way out before one of us faints. We will meet you two outside.'

Claire slowly got up from her seat, and together they made their way out of the gallery. James gestured towards the now-empty seat beside Mary. She nodded, and he took his place there. Moments later, Claire and Percy were in view below, braving a last look at the body before they made their way out into the refreshing night air. A small cry was promptly followed by the thud of a body hitting the ground.

'What the…?' James got up from his seat and peered over the balcony. 'Mary, Claire has fainted.'

There was the thud of another body hitting the ground. James glanced at Mary. 'And so has Percy.'

By the time Mary and James had caught up with Percy and Claire, they were huddled together on a wall outside, shivering against the cold.

'Do not ask me to go back in there,' Percy said with a shudder. 'I cannot.' He shook his head emphatically. Claire nodded her agreement; their hands were tightly gripped together.

Mary frowned. The dissection had been grim, of course, but surely it was not worthy of this response. She turned to look at Claire. 'Claire, do you feel the same way?' she asked.

'Nothing in Heaven or Hell could force me back in there.' She drew a long breath. 'There is a reason beyond the horror of what my eyes have just witnessed, which I have not the words to tell you here. Can we go home?'

'Home, yes, home,' Percy murmured.

Mary turned to James. 'I am sorry to cut short our evening. Please, go back inside. Come and see us on Sunday afternoon and tell me all that I have missed. Take notes, I will expect them!'

'Shall I help you all home?' James asked.

'No, thank you. We shall be all right,' Mary said with a smile. 'Goodnight, James.'

'Goodnight.' James bowed his head and walked back to the hall, opening the doors and releasing gasps and groans into the night air. Mary sighed inwardly. She had been looking forward to this night, and now she was to miss most of it. She wondered what all of their hearts would weigh at this moment; did a weak heart weigh less or more than a strong one? To be fair, she knew all about Percy's sensitive nature, but Claire's had come as more of a surprise. She drew them away from the building and down the cobbled road.

'Are we away from that frightful building?' Percy asked when they reached the lamp post by the corner. 'I am never setting foot in there again.'

'Nor I,' added Claire. 'I have much to say on the matter, but the city has as many ears as rivers and I do not wish my words to carry amongst them.'

Claire charged forward, causing Mary and Percy to break into a run to catch up with her. She kept up the pace all the way home and by the time they opened the front door, Mary was soaked with sweat and her calves were aflame.

'I know it is late, but I am possessed of a terrible thirst. Would anyone else like tea?' she asked when she had caught her breath.

'Tea would not calm me,' Claire replied, shaking her head. 'Have we anything stronger — whisky, perhaps? Or sherry?'

'I think I have some whisky,' Percy said, rushing around the room to find it. 'Here it is!' He held the bottle aloft like a trophy. 'I will pour our drinks while Mary makes the tea. Claire, can you gather all our notes pertaining to the case? I have something to add.'

Claire nodded. By the time she had gathered all the notes, Mary and Percy had returned with the drinks. She placed the notes on the table and picked up the glass, downing the whisky in one, coughing as she placed the empty glass down.

'That's better,' she replied.

'Are you going to tell me what frightened you so much?' Mary asked her, picking up her quill and dipping it into the ink.

Claire took a moment to compose herself, clenching her hands in front of her.

'Might a second drink help?' Percy asked, having finished his own, Mary noticed.

Claire nodded and Percy poured a second whisky.

'Thank you, Percy.' Claire sipped the drink this time. She seemed calmer. 'I think,' she began, 'I think that the man on the surgeon's table was the man I saw at the park.'

Mary gasped. 'The murderer?'

Claire nodded and took another sip of her whisky. 'I suspected it when they pulled the sheet back, but it was only when we went downstairs and I got a closer look — too close a look — that I was sure. His mouth had the same cruel twist, even in death.'

'You are *sure* of it?' asked Percy.

'As sure as I can be of a person half-seen in the darkness. The same fear washed over me, the same feeling I had when our eyes met in the park.'

'Then he has already been brought to justice.' Mary's shoulders sank. So much for their investigation; the Bow Street Runners must have solved the case right under their noses. But it had never been so much as mentioned in any of the dailies. How had she missed it all? It did not add up.

'I have seen no notices of public executions. Is there not notice of them?'

'Not all executions are public, Mary,' Percy replied.

'But there is an appetite for the public to watch the execution of a murderer. That is well known, is it not?'

Percy and Claire nodded.

'So if the murderer had been brought to justice, more swiftly than we could answer the case, then why is there no record of it? How has he gone from the gallows to the dissection table so swiftly?' Mary tapped the quill on her knee; she did not notice the trail of ink that marked her skirt.

Claire pointed. 'Mary, your skirt!'

'What? Oh!' Mary put the quill down and dabbed at the ink with her handkerchief, but only succeeded in smudging it further. Another skirt ruined. She would just have to soak it herself and hope for the best; the days of sending clothes out to washerwomen were long gone. Mary sighed. Some stains, like memories, could never be erased.

'That's it!' she suddenly cried. 'Percy, do you remember that book we read on the boat to France? About the latest discoveries about the heart? It was in French — you had to translate some of the denser medical terms?'

Percy nodded. 'Sénac? Yes, I remember it. Why?'

'If I remember correctly, it said something about blood settling in the lowest parts of the body after death, but only after six or seven hours. Do you remember that?'

'Vaguely.' Percy shook his head. 'I did not pay it that much attention.'

'Yet tonight, when the surgeon cut the body with the scalpel, it bled. It would not do that if it had been transported from an early morning gallows.'

'What are you saying, Mary?' Claire asked.

'I'm saying that there is no way that body came from the gallows.'

'So where did it come from?' Percy asked.

'That is what I intend to find out.' Mary took the quill and noted down the time, date and location of the public dissection, the names of the surgeons undertaking it and every other detail she could remember.

'Let me have another look at that likeness,' said Percy.

Mary shuffled through the paperwork until she landed once more on the picture Claire had sketched of the man she'd seen in the park.

Percy swallowed. 'You will recall I thought this man had a look of my tailor, Mr Hobbs? I was wrong, it wasn't my tailor. This man — the man lying dead on the surgeon's table — was my cobbler's assistant.' Percy slapped his hand against his forehead and sank back into his chair.

Pieces of news were like post chaises — nothing for days, then two came along at once. Mary could hardly take in this new information.

'Well, whoever he is, at least we know that he poses no danger to Claire. She cannot be hounded by a dead man,' Mary replied.

Claire shivered. 'It was strange to see him lying on the table like that, awaiting dissection.' She gulped. 'I know his insides better than his outsides.'

'It is very late.' Mary yawned. 'I think we will all benefit from a good night's sleep. We can contemplate our next steps in the morning when our minds are more equal to the task.'

Percy and Claire nodded their agreement. Mary put down the paper and quill and levered herself up from the chair. In the past two weeks her mobility had lessened considerably. She soothed her stomach with calm, circular motions and the baby fluttered beneath them.

Once they were in bed and the oil lamp left to its glowing night watch, Mary closed her eyes. Her body was heavy with fatigue, yet her mind continued to race despite her best efforts to quell it. Yawning herself into her slumber did nothing but bring the monster of her dreams, standing at the shoreline between wakefulness and sleep, waiting to consume her. Percy fidgeted beside her, his huffs and sighs confirming that sleep was proving elusive for him, too.

'Mary,' he whispered, 'are you still awake?'

'Yes, Percy. My mind will not quieten.'

'Nor mine. Mary…' He hesitated. 'Do you think less of me because of my fainting at the Surgeons' Hall? Has it made me less of a man in your eyes?'

Mary turned to face him. He was always so concerned about how he appeared to others, which seemed like a terrible contradiction for a man devoted to liberty.

'No, Percy, of course not. What makes you say that?'

'I am not a scholar like James Berry. I have squandered the last three months avoiding debt collectors and have written nothing of note or substance since Paris.'

'It has been a difficult time for you, Percy. It has been a difficult time for us all.'

Percy sighed. Mary wrapped her arms around him and pulled him to her. His familiar scent was as precious to her as any of the wonders of nature and every bit as glorious.

'It has been a time of much coming and going and idleness, but in these things there has been nothing but love, my darling, darling Percy.'

He kissed her and the spark between them was ignited once more; no further words were needed as their bodies gave the comfort that caused them to fall asleep in each other's arms and for Mary to feel, when she awoke the next morning, refreshed and whole — as if she had stepped back into a familiar state of loving that erased everything else.

'Good morning.' The morning light streamed through the curtains, illuminating Percy's features. With his pillowy lips and unruly curls, he looked like a cherub.

'Good morning to you, Mr Shelley.' Mary could not resist planting a kiss on his lips. He placed a hand on her back and pulled her into a lingering embrace that reminded her of the night before.

'I have missed being in your arms like this,' Percy sighed, stroking her hair.

'And I have missed being in your arms,' she replied. 'I wish we could stay here all day, but there are mysteries to be solved!' Mary slid out of his grasp. Her mind fizzed with renewed energy, but she knew her body would not accommodate such spontaneity. 'My mind feels sharp as a quill's nib — best to take advantage of it.'

Percy sighed heavily and sunk back onto the pillow. If he had been expecting a day of loving, he had underestimated her desire to solve this mystery. Her mind ran through everything they needed to do as she dressed — the people they needed to see, the questions they needed to ask. It was Saturday, when London was at its busiest. And where there was activity above, you could guarantee there would be more activity below and London's underworld would redouble their criminal efforts if there were richer pickings to be taken. It seemed like a capital night for Percy and James to follow Thomas Bell, if she could get a message to James.

'I do not suppose you have any idea where James might be this morning?'

'The doctor?' Percy scoffed. 'He will be lounging about in the coffee houses with the other scholars, sitting in the window probably, trying to catch the eye of the ladies going to the milliners or haberdashery.'

Mary smirked. 'Could you find him and bring him here? I want to talk him through the next stage of our plan.'

Percy, still in bed, rested his head on his arm. 'Plan, stages — this all sounds like a military operation, Mary. Are you our commander?' He raised an eyebrow. Mary could read the thoughts behind his expression and was not about to be drawn back into bed, as tempting as it was. Instead, she pouted and narrowed her eyes.

'Percy, you need to be serious. I need your help today; there are things you can do, places you can go that Claire and I cannot. You and James need to be our men in the field.'

Percy sighed loudly before sliding out of bed. 'Very well then, Mary. I shall get up and do your bidding.'

He moved with the slow and gracious movements of someone aware that they were being watched and equally aware that they were loved and desired by the person watching. Mary bit her lip as he walked towards her, mesmerised by the angles of his body. He stopped in front of her and smiled as he gently cupped her face in his hands and planted the lightest of kisses upon her lips.

'I will get dressed now and leave straight away,' he murmured.

Mary closed her eyes, breathing in the wave of desire that engulfed her.

'So I am to be civil to your friend Berry, am I? Not threaten him with pistols at dawn or a duel in your honour?'

'What?' The bubble of desire burst. 'Do not be so absurd, Percy. Civil you must be — there is no need for ridiculous manly displays of…' She hesitated. 'I do not even know why men do such foolish things as duels.'

'I do not think men know themselves, Mary. Often it is honour, respectability; regardless, it is fruitless. I told you I was shot at, didn't I?'

Mary smiled. 'Yes, you were targeted in Wales. Is that why you will never go back?' she asked sweetly. Knowing Percy's finances as intimately as she did, she suspected that the reason for his sudden departure from Wales had more to do with unpaid debts than ghosts with pistols.

'I will never again set foot in that heinous place,' said Percy forcefully.

'Well, you do not have to worry about it now, Percy. All you need to do is find James and bring him back here — if he is willing.'

Percy stepped towards her, fixing his buttons and tucking his shirt into his breeches. 'And if he is unwilling? Am I to bring him using coercion?'

'You are being most trying this morning, Percy. A good night's sleep has put you in a mischievous mood that is most unbecoming. I am trying to be serious and solve a mystery here!'

'And solve it you will, my love — that I know. Is Claire awake yet?'

'I have not heard her.'

'What will you do while you are waiting for me and Berry? I suppose you might enjoy a spot of needlework. Play a little piano.' It was Percy's turn to smirk. Mary looked around the room; it was just as well they were not entertaining any high society.

'I would happily entertain visitors if we had any to entertain. Have you forgotten, Percy, that we are social outcasts?'

'No, Mary, I have not forgotten and I am sorry for it; but now that my grandfather has softened his position towards me, an increase in my allowance will surely follow and then we will be set up. Where would you like to live?'

He swept her into his arms and she immediately forgot the momentary melancholy that had stained her mood.

'A house with more than two rooms and without a sour-faced landlady would be a start.' They laughed before she moved away from him. 'Right then, Percy,' she continued, serious once more. 'You find James and bring him back here. I shall wake Claire and ensure she is ready for a weekend of investigations. I am determined to find satisfaction before Christmas.'

'And if you can, what a gift that would be for everybody!' Percy kissed her on the forehead before picking up a biscuit from the plate on the table and making his way to the door. Mary laughed: he had tucked his coat-tails into his trousers.

# CHAPTER ELEVEN

Percy rounded his shoulders as he made his way into the coffee house. Even though the hour was early, the air was dense with smoke and filled with the loud, excited chatter of men with time on their hands and money in their pockets. No one gave him a second look as he passed their tables, but Percy still feared being recognised.

'Percy?' a voice cried out through the smoky haze. 'Over here.'

James Berry waved him over with a friendliness that made Percy grimace. Straightening himself up, he manufactured his own friendliness before responding.

'There you are! I've been looking all over town for you. Are you busy?'

'And a very good morning to you, too.' James, seated with similarly dressed fellows, had seemed to acquire their habits too.

'Mary wishes to see you. Are you available to come with me now?'

James frowned. 'Is she unwell?'

'No, nothing like that. It pertains to matters I cannot discuss here, but I will happily divulge them if you come with me.'

James finished his coffee before bidding his companions farewell and following Percy outside. As they walked, Percy resumed their conversation.

'Mary is keen to dissect last night's events. She could not wait until tomorrow.'

'I see. And are you fully recovered now?'

Percy flushed. 'I am well,' he snapped. 'It was not the matter of the dissection that made me unwell, but the remembrances it brought with it.' A half-lie, but James didn't need to know that.

'Remembrances?' James had quickened his pace, and Percy matched it.

'I knew the man on the table. That is all I am prepared to say on the matter until we have reached Mary. All will be revealed when we arrive.'

The early morning air was rich with the smell of freshly baked bread from the baker's shops, and Percy's stomach rumbled.

'I have not eaten yet,' said James. 'Do you suppose Mary would mind if I brought breads and pastries?'

'We have food of our own,' Percy retorted, though he knew it was insufficient for their own needs, let alone those of a guest. 'But you must do as you wish if you are hungry. I will wait outside the shop for you.' Percy folded his arms. James trotted into the shop, flooding Percy's senses with the smells from the open door. It would be Christmas in a few weeks and although he was no longer hounded by the ghosts of his former debts, he was still poor and with no immediate hope of gathering money. A different life taunted his mind, one in which he had not got sent down from Oxford and had continued his medical training. He was not so much older than Berry; he could have been a surgeon by now, and all this scrapping around for food like birds on a barren winter's branch would be nothing but imagination.

James returned with a large box wrapped in brown paper. 'Ready.' He smiled and they walked on in silence.

By the time they reached Nelson Square Claire had risen. She greeted Percy with a hug and James with a curt nod which made Percy smirk.

'That dissection last night has given me an appetite.' James smiled, putting the box down on the table.

'Really? Even the thought of it turns my stomach.' Claire wrinkled her nose, but her eyes remained trained on the box and she licked her lips once the treasures inside were revealed.

'Are you bringing in plates and tea, Mary?' Claire called.

Percy looked at Mary, who shook her head and got up from her seat. He sank down into the vacated space, soothed by her warmth underneath him. He allowed his shoulders to relax now they were home; there was nothing to fear here, no knocks at the door, no unwelcome intrusions. He could even tolerate James Berry on his own terrain.

'Percy, can you help me here?' Mary appeared in the doorway, attempting to juggle plates, cups and a teapot on an unruly tray.

'Certainly.' He shot up from the seat, took the tray from her and put it down on the table.

'What a feast!' Mary's eyes shone as she surveyed the pastries. 'You are very kind, James, bringing us treats like this.'

The smile that passed between Mary and James pierced Percy's heart and reopened an old wound — the feeling that he was not good enough for her. Sadness washed over him anew and stole his appetite.

'Percy,' Mary said, 'are you not eating?'

He shook his head. 'I am not hungry, Mary, but I will take tea if it is on offer?'

She poured him a cup of tea and passed it over with a smile and a steady hand. He stared at her face, comparing the smiles and the meaning behind them. It was all in his head; there was nothing but friendliness from Mary. They did not have many friends, so it stood to reason that she should be keen to keep the ones they had.

'Are you daydreaming, Percy?' Claire asked.

Her words brought his attention back to the room. The conversation had resumed without him and Mary and Claire had brought James up to speed with the fact that Claire had recognised the man on the dissecting table as being the murderer in the park.

'But that is not all, James. Percy thinks he knows the identity of the murderer, don't you, Percy?'

'What? Oh, yes, yes, I do.' Percy coughed. All eyes were trained upon him, and the weight of expectation made the hairs on the back of his neck prickle. 'I believe — and I am not entirely sure, mind — that he might be my cobbler's assistant.'

James turned swiftly to Mary. 'Well, that would explain the shoes on the bench outside the workshop. It must be used for something illegal, but what?'

'Smuggling is my guess,' replied Percy. The rumble in his stomach returned and he swallowed his pride in readiness to swallow something more substantial. He picked up a pastry and consumed it in one delicious bite. 'The post chaise leaves from the tavern half a league from the shops. It would not be so difficult to move a chest from there to the river.'

'And if it was being transported upriver, where would it be going? What commodity could it be?' James asked.

'Anywhere.' Percy shrugged. 'Anywhere the goods are needed.'

'But it is possible that the goods never leave the country, that they are transported from one place to another? Surely there must be as much trade in that?' James picked up a pastry and waved it in the air as he spoke.

'Our next actions are simple.' Mary spoke firmly. 'Claire, you need to write a note to Thomas Bell asking him to meet you tomorrow at Richmond Park at noon. We shall deliver the note. Percy, you need to buy work clothes and the orange necktie worn by Thomas Bell's gang. There is only one way we are going to get to the bottom of this — you are going to join them.'

Once they had left the note at Bell's lodgings, Mary was in no mood to be social, so they made their way back through the Lambeth marshes to the safety of Nelson Square. Knowing that the murderer was now committed to several jars and a pile of ash in the Royal College of Surgeons had put a fresh spring in Claire's step. Mary bit her lip; she could not share her sister's elevated mood. There was no peace of mind in not knowing who the woman in the park was, or what had happened to her. If they could uncover any proof of criminality, then they could get the Bow Street Runners involved. But proof was thin on the ground; all they had were speculations that evaporated as quickly as mist.

They walked back through the open spaces where the skyline and London met, meandering slowly through the quiet winter's day. Everything seemed slower in the winter; the cooling temperature calmed the London streets until life crawled at a snail's pace. Next winter, Mary would be pushing a baby in a pram. She tried to picture herself as a mother, the gentle warmth of a child's body giving her a new sense of purpose. She was almost breathless with the changes of the past year. Just over a year earlier, she had been a schoolgirl in Scotland, reading romances with a Gothic twist, and now here she was, living one. Regret twisted in her stomach. She wished her father and Mary Jane would forgive her; this would be the first

Christmas she had spent without them, and Mary couldn't contemplate going into the next year, and a new chapter in her life, without them. Mary Jane's love was no loss, as it had never truly been given, but her father's was another story. She had been the centre of his world until Mary Jane's arrival. Her stepmother's campaign of flattery and seduction had been so intense that no man could have resisted it. Once he had married her, there had seemed to be no space left in his heart for his daughter, as if she were nothing more than an artefact from his former marriage, to be put away and ignored. Mary stroked her stomach. She would never behave that way; this child would always feel loved, nurtured and supported, no matter what happened.

It was late afternoon by the time they returned. Mary was glad they had enjoyed such an elaborate meal in the morning, for there was nothing but parsnips for tea. They would make a weak soup, if nothing else, and at least it would soften the stale bread that would accompany it. The gas lamps outside burst into flame as the dull afternoon fell into evening. Mary opened the front door and saw two gentlemen standing in the hallway outside their rooms.

'Mary Godwin? Claire Clairmont?' the taller of the two men asked.

Panic overwhelmed Mary. She swallowed, trying to find her voice. 'Has something happened to Percy?' she cried.

The two men introduced themselves as Inspector Johnson and Sergeant Green. 'We are here to talk to you about a missing person.' The tall man, Sergeant Green, had a moustache that twitched up at the corners when he spoke.

'A missing person?' Mary echoed, ushering them into the apartment.

'Yes, Mrs Eleanor Knapp.'

Mary stared at them, then gestured for them to sit down.

'Thank you.' Inspector Johnson pulled out a notebook. 'We were alerted to her absence last night, and your names were given to us as people who might know something about it. The neighbours remembered you visiting her.'

'Why on earth would we know anything about it?' Claire asked defensively.

Mary put her hand on Claire's wrist. 'Perhaps you would arrange us some tea, Claire?'

Claire huffed as she left the room. Now she was out of the way, Mary could sort this out.

'When did you last see Mrs Knapp?' Inspector Johnson asked.

'Only a day or two ago. She used to work for my father and we have remained friendly.'

'Did she mention that she was going away?'

'Not that I recall.' Mary frowned. 'She has a sister in Hampshire, I think. Perhaps she has gone to visit her?'

'Is it likely she would leave her lodgings without a word to anyone?' Sergeant Green asked.

'No.' Mary swallowed.

Claire returned with the tea just as the gentlemen stood up to leave.

'We won't take up any more of your time, Miss Godwin,' Inspector Johnson said. 'We might need to call on you again.'

'Of course, anything we can do to help.'

Johnson clicked his fingers and Green passed him a calling card. 'Here's where we're based, should anything else come to mind.'

Mary took the card and nodded. 'I hope Mrs Knapp is found safely.'

She closed the door and let out a breath she hadn't realised she had been holding.

Claire was staring at her. 'Mrs Knapp is in trouble, isn't she?'

'Yes, I fear so. We need to try and find her.'

Percy and James had hidden themselves behind a barrel opposite Thomas Bell's lodgings. Night had closed in around them, the moon casting patches of light to guide them. Percy felt something move beside his foot and a cat shrieked as it fled from their hiding place.

'There he is!' hissed James, crouched beside Percy.

Thomas Bell strolled out of his lodgings, oil lamp in hand.

'Come on, if we do not hurry, we will lose him.'

Percy uncurled himself away from the barrel and followed James into the night. Both men were dressed in casual work clothes and matching orange neckties.

They followed the small orange glow of the oil lamp and were close enough to catch the tune Thomas whistled as he walked. It was a romantic ballad that had been popular a year earlier. *Perhaps he's thinking about Claire*, Percy thought to himself, then he immediately hoped not.

Thomas carried on, past the taverns and up through the marshes. The countryside fell away as tall, black buildings appeared against the skyline. Harsh shadows gave no clues to the buildings' daytime faces, and all Percy could be sure of was that they had walked some miles through the city, cutting a path alongside the slums.

'Is this Bethnal Green?' Percy whispered.

'I think so,' James replied.

His voice was louder than Percy's and he had answered without care. Thomas swung around and raised the lamp high. The light illuminated his features as he peered into the night.

'Is anyone there?' Thomas called. 'If you are, you had better show yourself before I find you.'

A sliver of silver glinted in the darkness. Percy gulped. Thomas Bell was armed with a knife.

They held their breath as Thomas menacingly slashed the winter night with the knife, before turning and continuing on, obviously content that he was alone. They passed one dark corner after another, each indistinguishable from the last.

'He's stopping.' James thrust out his arm, preventing Percy from going forward. Percy looked ahead, blinking into the darkness. Thomas had entered a derelict shed, leaving his oil lamp at the entrance. They could hear movement inside and took the opportunity to get closer. James nodded towards the side of the shed, where they could hide in the shadows. Thomas reappeared with a wooden shovel, putting it down while he locked the door and picked up his lamp. He walked off, whistling again.

'He's picked up a shovel,' Percy whispered. 'Quick, we're losing him.'

Thomas had been joined by two other men, all carrying some sort of tool — one appeared to be a crowbar and the other a long tool with a curved top, perhaps a scythe? It was hard to be sure in the darkness. Thomas certainly seemed merry enough with these other men; they were laughing and joking. Though the objects in their hands were all different, one thing bonded the men together — an orange necktie.

'We cannot join them. We have no implements,' Percy whispered.

James nodded. 'If we attempt to join them now, they may use those tools on us.'

'What are they doing?' Percy asked as the motley crew made their way towards the graveyard.

James gulped. 'I have an idea.'

Slowly, they followed the men, using the shadow of the graveyard wall to conceal themselves. A short whistle was given by the man with the scythe, and Thomas set his lamp atop a fresh mound of earth topped by a small wooden cross and sheltered by the branches of a tree.

'Why has he put the lamp there?' Percy asked. 'Will it not illuminate the scene for all to see?'

Percy looked around and deduced the answer to his own question. Apart from the three men and themselves — hiding behind the wall — they were quite alone.

Thomas wiped his forehead with his necktie; it caught the glow of the lamp like a stray flame. The shovel was heavy with soil.

The lamplight illuminated the faces of the two other men — an older man with a weathered face was holding the scythe; the other, a shorter, younger man, had the crowbar. Thomas Bell made up the third in this unholy trinity.

The sound of metal against wood drifted through the air. Soon it was followed by grunts and groans as the men exerted themselves in physical labour, their backs hunched like snail shells.

'Pull it up to the surface,' came a man's voice through the darkness. It was followed by renewed grunts as a coffin was lugged up and placed at the side of the open crevice. The sound of wood splintering echoed through the air, and then a flash of white was briefly illuminated by the lamp's glow — long enough for Percy to see that it was a pair of feet which were then pulled from the coffin by two of the men.

The sound of soil hitting wood told him that they were reburying an empty coffin. Percy bowed his head, his heart heavy with sorrow for the family and friends of the deceased, who might have thought that putting a cross on the grave would prevent a scene like this. *How willing we are to look for the good in people*, he thought, *and how reluctant we are to see the shadows in men's hearts*. Percy turned his attention back to the scene as the body was carried away from the grave by the two men, one lifting under the arms, another taking the legs. They laid the body on the ground beside the tree, where it stayed while they finished filling the grave with soil.

Percy and James ducked behind the wall as Thomas walked past, then watched as his faithful lamp spotlighted his route up to a shed set back from the graveyard. He opened it and returned with something rolled under his arm and a wheeled trolley — the sort used to transport crates of fruit. He whistled softly back through the graveyard, the wheels grinding against the stones.

'Reckon we'll get a good price for this one.' The two men had completed their task: one scurried around collecting tools, while the other helped Thomas to get the body into the sack he had unrolled from under his arm.

'Straight to Hosier for this one.' A younger voice this time, one they had not heard before.

'Fool! You want to shout out the number as well?' It was the older man's angry voice. 'Tell the cart to meet us at the corner.'

The lad ran out of the graveyard with an urgency that suggested he was new to this role. Still, he was quick and soon disappeared into the darkness.

'Hosier?' Percy whispered to James. 'What's that?'

'I presume they mean Hosier Lane. It is not far from here.'

'Then why have they summoned a horse and cart?'

'They can hardly walk around Smithfield with a body without arousing suspicion, can they? A horse and cart will conceal the cargo until they reach their destination. If we cut over those fields, we can reach Hosier Lane before they do. We can traverse the stiles and kissing gates — a horse cannot.'

Percy shuddered. 'If we get there alive in this frosty darkness, it will be a miracle.'

'And if we do not, they will have two more bodies for their collection.'

By the time James and Percy reached Hosier Lane, they were as hot as summer.

'They cannot be bringing it here. There is nothing but shops and businesses,' said Percy, trying to catch his breath. He scanned the dark street. There was no glimpse of life, no movement but that of the rodents scuttling behind bags of rubbish. The businesses on this south side of the city mirrored those to be found at any of London's other compass points — tailors, quill makers, bakers, butchers. There was nothing to distinguish this area from any of London's other commercial districts.

'Do not forget that our investigation led us to a cobbler's workshop last time; it could be any one of these places. I'll stay here; you go behind and see if there are any outbuildings.' James's voice had an authority that Percy did not question, and he scuttled off to seek the backs of the businesses.

James kept watch at the front, shivering in the darkness now that his heart had stopped racing. As a medical student he had heard whispers of resurrectionists but had never dreamt that such things were real. The other students had laughed over jugs of ale at the bodies brought in for dissection; one fellow had even recognised a woman as being a street walker he had recently invested in, but James had presumed they had all met criminal ends — their bodies legally conveyed to the anatomists following execution for murder — not that they had been dug up for the dissection table. There was so much that was unrespectable about the profession, its status elevated to a societal pedestal that it rarely deserved; still, he was not the one to rock the boat — not when he had secrets enough of his own to conceal.

James's attention was drawn to the sound of horses' hooves on the cobbles. A black cart wound its way through the street and stopped outside a house set back on the corner of the road. James crouched down and crept closer. A large oak tree shielded him from view while providing him with an excellent position from which to watch the proceedings. The house was in darkness. A lamp post outside provided no light, and James reasoned the lamp had been taken out. This told him two things: firstly, that this was not the first time this had happened, and secondly, that the person inside the house was as culpable for the crime as the men carrying the body from the cart.

Thomas came into view, his oil lamp waning, offering little more than a flicker of light to confirm his identity. The lamp was discarded at the side of the road. Once the body was free of the cart, it too disappeared, taking its unknown driver with it. All James had seen was the silhouette of a man in a dark coat and hat drawn low over his features — hardly enough to give a description to the Runners. Thomas tapped at the front door of the house and James shifted so he could better see the doorway.

A man opened the door and James caught a glimpse of the interior of the house. The hallway was grand, much grander than the exterior; perhaps it had been chosen for its duplicity.

Thomas and the other men carried the body inside. Once again, his whistle scratched at the air and James's skin prickled with irritation at the straightforward manner in which Thomas could undertake this task, as if he were doing nothing more than taking out the rubbish or moving rolls of haberdashery from one place to another. The body was transported into the house; the man who had opened the door passed something to the older man and the group disbanded like a flock of ravens taking flight.

Percy appeared just as Thomas was walking away. Once Thomas had passed, James gestured to get his attention. Percy made his way over to him.

'They took the body into that house.' James pointed. 'Let's take a closer look.'

They crossed the road, now restored to its peaceful state. It seemed incredible that only moments earlier it had been the site of such macabre deeds.

James stared up at the dark windows. 'There's something odd about this house.'

'The windows are blacked out,' Percy replied. 'Someone has painted them.'

Percy had insisted on seeking a tavern to discuss all they had witnessed. James had been reluctant but agreed that he too needed a drink to stabilise his thoughts.

They walked to The Mermaid on the corner of the road. Opening the door to the smoky tavern, all eyes turned towards them and the noisy chatter that had rolled through the interior just moments earlier was replaced by silence. A barmaid at the counter was the first to speak.

'Are they Blaze's men?' she whispered to a man hunched over a stool. James and Percy could not fail to hear her harsh words.

The man at the bar turned to look at them, then turned back to the bar.

'Looks like.' He sniffed, burying his nose in his tankard.

James turned to Percy. 'We forgot to take off our neckties,' he hissed. 'They think we're a part of it.'

The barmaid approached them, her arms folded. 'Is he with you?' she asked. 'He's not been in for a while.'

Percy and James exchanged a nervous glance. 'No,' Percy ventured.

'I suppose you've been up to St Giles.' She moved closer, her eyes narrowed. 'Hands,' she ordered. 'There'll be no soil on my tankards.'

Percy and James held out their hands. The woman snatched them, holding them up for rigorous scrutiny.

She frowned. 'There's not a scrap of dirt on your hands. What did you say your names were?'

'Hattie, a drink, or have you joined the Bow Street Runners now?'

The sound of a tankard slapping the side of the bar dragged her gaze away from them, and as she turned her back to see to her customer, Percy and James scuttled out of the tavern and back into the biting night air.

'We should have taken the neckties off.' Percy fumbled to untie the orange scarf, but it became knotted. 'Blaze's men can be identified by them.'

'Here, let me.' James untied Percy's necktie. Percy realised that the same flash of fear that he felt had besieged James; perhaps they were not so different after all.

'Do you need help with yours?' Percy stuffed the scarf into his jacket pocket.

'No, mine is not tied as tight as yours.' James untied his with one hand. 'Perhaps you have forgotten how they teach you to tie them at medical school.'

Percy sighed. 'I have forgotten a good many things in my short life. If a thought is not important to me, I do not allow myself to become encumbered by it. Often, I forget even all that I should remember.' He yawned, fatigue suddenly wrapping itself around him like a blanket.

'Perhaps it might be safer to take a drink at my lodgings. Mine are much closer than yours, and I want to be certain that I have fully understood everything that has passed this evening.'

The bells had pealed midnight several hours since, and Percy's body was heavy and stiff. Happily, James's lodgings were quickly found and Percy yawned his way up the stairs, incurring shushing gestures from James, who pointed towards a closed door from which the sound of heavy snores rumbled. 'My landlady,' he whispered.

Moments later, Percy clutched a glass of sherry as if embracing a beloved friend. The liquid slid down his throat with a familiar warmth that banished the winter chill from his bones. He closed his eyes and sighed contentedly.

'That is better.' He smiled and drained the glass.

'Another?' James asked. Percy nodded and tipped the glass towards him. James laughed as he replenished the glass, leaving the bottle on the table.

'Can I ask you something?' Percy scrambled to sit up straight in his chair. 'Did you suspect they might be resurrectionists?'

James shook his head. 'Though I have studied in London, I'm afraid I have kept much of my countryside naivety.' He hesitated. 'Of course I have heard of such things, but I confess I have given little thought to it. I would not have thought such things were possible had I not witnessed it with my own eyes. I am sure that if we go back at daybreak, we will see some sign of their endeavour.'

Percy clicked his fingers, an idea quickly forming in his mind. 'Have you got some paper and ink? We must commit all the details to paper before the sherry numbs the edges.'

James rushed around his room, pushing books off a desk until he brandished a sheet of paper in the air. 'Found one!'

'Capital. So, we need to tell Mary that there were three of them — one being Thomas Bell, an older man who could have been this Blaze character and a younger lad who seemed more like a runner than anything else. We know the graveyard was on the south side and the house where the body was delivered was in… Where was it again?'

'Hosier Lane,' James replied.

'Right. Hosier Lane. And it was delivered to a gentleman, though I don't know of any gentleman with blacked-out windows in their houses.'

'A gentleman who does not wish his business to be seen?'

Percy nodded. 'Certainly. So, here is what I propose we do next: we go to the house — if he is a God-fearing man, then he will attend the first church service of the day, despite his nocturnal activities. But we must go to the graveyard before then, at first light, to see if there are any signs of disturbance. Have you got all that, James?'

The gentle snoring coming from the opposite chair confirmed that James had not. Percy gently levered himself out of his own chair, took the paper and quill from James's hands and wrote down his notes. He folded the sheet of paper and put it in his pocket before scanning the room for a blanket or coat to put over James's slumbering body. Finding two, he put one over James and then settled back down into his chair, deciding that he might as well have a quick nap himself.

Percy closed his eyes and his mind drifted to Mary. It was calming to consider the curve of her eyelids and the chestnut eyes that rested beneath them, with all the wisdom and wonder they held. He mentally traced the bridge of her nose and the soft flow of her lips, which greeted him with a gentle smile that instantly soothed his spirits. Mary felt like home and had set a standard for companionship that made his soul ache and turned all thoughts of Harriet to stone.

Thoughts of their life together ran like rivers through his mind. Every favourable moment he had known had Mary at its centre. Percy pictured the wide-open spaces of Paris with the poetry and power of the Left Bank resting as hazily on the air as the red wine fumes. The heat and sweat seemed bound to a different time, not just a different season. Percy raised a hand to his eyes and squinted. It was morning and the blazing sun he had dreamt of had been the light streaming in through James's open curtains. A Sunday morning crowd were reverentially making their way down the street, attired in their best bonnets and skirts, the men with hair brushed a lick neater than on other days. He had rested far longer than he had intended.

'James! James, wake up.' Percy shook the chair. James reluctantly stirred. 'We fell asleep. We need to get to the graveyard before the church service ends. Come on, quickly.'

Percy and James rushed out of the apartment, joining the swelling throng of people on their way to church. Their destination being a different church, they left the crowd at the end of the road and ran over the fields that provided the same shortcut they had taken hours earlier. The winter sun had won out against the frosts and the ground was moist as they made their way back to the graveyard. It was easy to find the grave again as Percy remembered the tree. The stone faces of angels and cherubs seemed harsher in the daylight, more judgemental, and Percy bowed his head as he made his way past them towards the twice-dug grave.

'There's nothing to see.' Percy shook his head, astonished that the gravediggers had left no trace of their disturbance. To the untrained eye, it looked as if the grave had not been touched since the body had been laid in the ground.

'Not on the grave itself, but look here.'

To the side of the grave, where the feet of the corpse had briefly rested the previous night, there was a square patch of flattened grass that could be a sign of intrusion.

'Every criminal leaves behind a clue.'

# CHAPTER TWELVE

'I suppose a lady must always have a chaperone,' Thomas said with a smile that emphasised his rotten teeth.

Claire attempted a smile, but it was soured by the bile that rose in her throat. She waved a weak hand at Mary, who had positioned herself on the bench in front of the lake. *Some lookout Mary is*, Claire thought to herself. *She has her eyes closed.* She breathed in deeply, gave an infinitely more convincing smile than the first, and allowed Thomas to take her arm and walk her through the park.

Knowing that the murderer had been apprehended and was no more should have brought a sense of relief, but the victory felt hollow; there was still so much that she wanted to know. Claire doubted that they'd ever know the truth of it.

'This is the second time we have walked out now, Claire,' said Thomas. Though Claire had softened towards him, she would never make peace with those teeth. 'People will start to talk about us.'

'People are quick to talk and very slow to listen.' Claire hesitated. 'Speaking of which, I would like to know more about you, Thomas. Tell me about your family.'

'Not much to tell.' He scuffed the ground in front of him with his shoe. 'Ran away from home as soon as I could; my sister Annie wasn't far behind.' His eyes glistened. 'It's a hard life and no mistaking, but at least it is all my own and I can come and go as I please.'

'Where is Annie now?'

'I don't know. When Mrs Knapp said she'd give her work, I thought we'd struck gold, but when she told me she had upped and disappeared during the night, well, it grieves me to think on it, to be honest with you.'

Claire frowned. 'Mrs Knapp told you she'd disappeared?'

'Yes,' he replied. 'Why else would she clear her room and give me her stuff?'

Claire's heart beat a warning drum in her chest. 'Let me get this straight. Annie — your sister — worked for Mrs Knapp, who then told you that she'd gone missing and gave you her belongings?'

'Yes. I thought you knew all that?'

Claire looked up at the opal winter sky, her thoughts racing. Mrs Knapp had let them think that Thomas knew all about Annie's disappearance and was trying to cover something up. But what if it were the other way around? What if Mrs Knapp knew all about Annie's disappearance and Thomas knew nothing?

'I do not really know Mrs Knapp. She worked for my stepfather before he married my mother. She is more of an acquaintance of Mary's than mine.' Claire hesitated, then asked, 'What do you know of her?'

Thomas wiped his nose with his sleeve, making Claire wince.

'Always seemed fair to me — kind to her lodgers, always giving them food, that sort of thing.' He paused. 'Seemed to have quite a lot of them, but that's London for you, ain't it? People expect to find streets of gold, not streets of dirt.'

'How long have you known her?'

'Ever since I started at the butchers, almost as long as I've been here. Two years, give or take.'

'And your sister Annie?'

'She's had a few jobs. Thought she'd landed on her feet when she got a job in a big house, but it wasn't to last. That was her last position before she worked for Mrs Knapp.'

'What happened?'

'They accused her of stealing. Our Annie, who'd never stolen so much as a glance in her life. I always reckoned the man of the house had taken a liking to her and the wife didn't like it.'

Claire stopped, suddenly aware that she had been so distracted by the conversation that she hadn't kept Mary in sight and they had walked deep into the recesses of the park. Her body stiffened. It remembered the spot where the murder had taken place before she did.

'Did Annie get on well with Mrs Knapp?' Claire asked, fighting the urge to run away.

'Annie thought the world of her. Mrs Knapp was very handy to us both.'

'How has Mrs Knapp been handy to you?' Claire shook her head. 'I don't understand.'

'Got me hooked up with a job too, didn't she? You saw the scarf in my room — you know what it means. We've been in *The Newgate Calendar* and everything — not that I can read it, mind.'

Claire tried desperately to keep up with the information he was giving her. It was overwhelming.

'Mrs Knapp gave you the scarf? Is that what you are saying?'

Thomas stared at her blankly. 'Are you dicked in the nob?' He chuckled as he tapped his forehead. 'She gets all the runners for Blaze's mob.'

Claire put a hand to her mouth as a wave of dizziness swept over her. Mrs Knapp? Could that kindly old woman really have something to do with it? It occurred to her that she had never actually shown Thomas the picture of the man she had seen in the park that night and pulled a copy of the sketch from her bag.

'I don't suppose you recognise this man?'

Thomas took the piece of paper from Claire and studied it. The colour drained from his face. 'Is this some sort of a joke?' The paper shook in his hands. 'Why are you showing me a picture of Jack Cotton?'

Claire resisted the temptation to tell him that the man was already dead and that his body had been dissected at the Royal College of Surgeons.

'Do you know him?' Claire asked, keen to know why the picture had caused such a violent response.

'Yes, I've known him for years. Why?' Thomas asked.

Claire sighed. It was time to tell him the full story.


It was midday before Percy and James made their way back to Nelson Square. Percy's stomach was empty and his throat parched; he prayed there was something to eat in the house as he had no money to purchase anything and was reluctant to rely on James's generosity.

Mary and Claire were not at home but had left a note alongside a loaf of bread and some biscuits, which Percy made short work of.

James picked up the note. 'They have gone to keep their date with Thomas Bell in Richmond Park.'

The two men exchanged a look. Mary and Claire had no knowledge of Thomas's nocturnal activities.

'Then that is where we must go too,' Percy replied firmly.

'It is useless. By the time we get there on foot, they will have gone.'

'Then we must get ourselves some horses.'


Mary heard the sound of hooves as she made her way to the island. Having stopped to help a child retrieve a ball, she had lost sight of Claire and Thomas. Why had she been so foolish as to let Claire go with him alone? She should have insisted on taking every step with them. Never in her life had she been more thankful when she spied Percy and James atop the horses like a pair of watchmen.

'Thank goodness it is you two.' She sighed, her body relaxing at the sight of reinforcements. A pregnant woman could do little more than waddle in the face of adversity. 'I've lost them — I think they may have gone to the island.'

James jumped down from his horse, then helped Mary up into the saddle. He climbed back in front of her and she placed her hands around his waist. Mary noticed Percy shoot James a haughty glare as they cantered off, but as he had not got off his horse or offered her a space, he had very little right of recourse; she was just glad that she was no longer navigating the park alone. Mary shuddered at the thought of how many foul deeds may have been committed in the park and how many went unnoticed or lay buried beneath the turf.

'Over there, I can see her.'

In the distance, Mary saw Thomas pacing up and down. Claire looked like she was trying to appease him. Relief, like a welcome ray of sunshine, spread through her body.

'She is unharmed. Thank goodness for that.'

It was Claire who noticed them first. She turned and put her hand to her chest. 'Thank goodness you're here.'

Mary rushed towards her, enveloping her in a hug hindered by her swollen stomach.

'Did you think yourself in danger, Claire?' Thomas spluttered, scanning the faces of the unwelcome intruders. 'I do not understand. What is happening?' He stopped and stared at James. 'You.' He pointed towards him. 'You have been following me. I saw you last night at the graveyard.'

'Mary, Claire.' Percy took their hands and drew them away from Thomas. 'You need to get away from this man. He is dangerous.'

'Dangerous?' Mary echoed. 'Dangerous how?'

'We thought he might be smuggling spices or ale, Mary, but his crimes are far more heinous than that. He is a resurrectionist.'

'You left me with a *resurrectionist*?' cried Claire in a shrill voice.

'At least he had the decency to scarper,' Percy replied.

Thomas had turned on his heel and swiftly left when Percy had revealed his profession. Together they rode the horses back to Nelson Square, where a hot, sweet cup of tea was needed to digest the shock of everything they had learnt.

'So, alongside running errands, Thomas is also a member of Blaze's gang of grave robbers?' Mary sighed and put down the quill. 'I am going to need more ink.'

'He informed Claire that Mrs Knapp had put him onto it,' added Percy.

Claire nodded and picked up her teacup. 'And apparently it was Mrs Knapp who informed him of Annie's disappearance and packed up her belongings.'

'Mrs Knapp has been leading us a merry dance from the start. It is just as well we did not secure you a position or lodgings with her — she is not to be trusted.' Mary was shocked; she had known Mrs Knapp and would have sworn to her moral character. Her heart twisted at the idea of being fooled by someone she had trusted.

'I find it hard to believe that men of science would be involved in any of this,' James said despondently.

Percy shrugged. 'Science is advancing at such a pace that the gallows cannot keep up with the demand for bodies. Where there is demand for cadavers in medical education and research, there will be criminals willing to illegally exhume them.'

'Tell me once again about the men. Did you say there were three?' Mary picked up the quill. 'An elder who may or may not be called Blaze? Thomas Bell, and a third, a young lad who kept watch?'

Percy nodded. 'That is correct.'

'And, Claire, you know from Thomas that Mrs Knapp put him in contact with them?'

'Yes.' Claire nodded. 'Then I showed him the likeness of the man from the park and it sent him into a rage.'

Mary tapped her lips with the quill. 'Mrs Knapp told us that Annie disappeared without a word, that lately she'd had a terrible time keeping staff.' She paused. 'Percy, what do you know of the cobbler's assistant?'

'Not much. He was called Jack; he was often in the tavern. He enjoyed gambling. You could always tell how well or badly he'd fared at the bookies by the way he shined the shoes.' Percy stopped to mimic a frantic brushing movement.

'Jack is the name Thomas shouted in the park. Jack Cotton. Do you think it is likely that the cobbler is somehow involved too?'

They fell silent as each tried to find an answer to Mary's question. She noticed a spiderweb, surprised to see it shimmering in the corner of the ceiling. A spider with long, transparent legs was making a getaway. Mary scribbled down the question. It was foolish to expect answers to come all at once; a mystery was like a web, winding and intricate.

'Perhaps the crate you saw being taken away from the workshop was another body, but that one went towards the dock?'

James nodded. 'Yes, the carriage headed in that direction.'

'And the removal of the newly buried body last night — that was delivered to the house on Hosier Lane with the blacked-out windows?'

Percy nodded this time.

'So, we have one trip going from south to east — Lambeth to Hosier, and the first from west to water. What can we learn from that?' Mary scratched her head. 'Why are they choosing these routes?'

'I've got it.' James punched the air. 'The two routes you have described both have graveyards, shops, horse-paths and rivers, so they can move the bodies from the graveyards and hide them in sheds or outbuildings, before transporting them to…' He paused. 'To wherever they are going.'

'It was the orange neckties that made the barmaid ask if we were Blaze's men, so it is safe to assume that he frequents taverns, though I believe he had not been in The Mermaid of late.'

'Each route has taverns, graveyards, shops, horse-paths and rivers. Right.' Mary exhaled. 'That is quite a list of requirements.'

'Unfortunately, there are many places like that in London. We could not hope to cover all of them.'

'No,' Mary agreed. 'We couldn't. But we can keep watch on the house in Hosier Lane and follow Thomas Bell again; he may lead us to Blaze.' Mary paused and surveyed the faces of those she loved and trusted. 'Uncovering the truth could put us all in harm's way. There are dangerous people involved. Do we carry on and bring the grave-robbing gang down, or do we stop it here, absolve ourselves of everything we have uncovered and carry on as if we have learnt nothing?'

The silence in the room stretched. Mary reflected on all that had happened since the row with Percy over the scribblings in her journal; Percy's wild interest in Charles had dwindled once the battle to see him had been overcome, her own pregnancy had swelled, a new friendship with James had been forged and it appeared an old friendship with Mrs Knapp had been built on a stack of lies. The axis of her life was tilting again, and there was only so much uncertainty she could take before she sickened with the constant motion of it all. In that moment, Mary longed to be back in her former life, back at the school in Scotland where she had nothing more pressing to do than school lessons, no decisions to make other than which book to read next. She craved the simplicity of those earlier summers she had enjoyed, which now seemed a lifetime away. The baby kicked its disapproval and Mary was reminded that these decisions had been hers. *This is the life I chose.* Mostly, it was agreeable to her, but she was tired, hungry and out of her depth and needed a strength that at that moment she did not possess.

'We must keep going until we have all the answers.' James nodded decisively.

'Is that how you all feel?' Mary looked at Percy and Claire, who both nodded their assent. 'Then we carry on until we have uncovered the truth.'

# CHAPTER THIRTEEN

'There, that is as much as I can remember.' Claire put down the pencil. 'And please don't ask me to see Thomas Bell again to see if this sketch is a true likeness; I will not walk out with him.'

Mary knew they'd already asked too much of Claire. There would be safety in numbers; from now on they would go everywhere together.

'All we need to do is confirm some link between the men in your two pictures, then we will know what happened to the woman.'

'And Mrs Knapp? What are we to do about her?'

Mary shrugged. 'Perhaps she has returned now, or perhaps finding this man, Blaze, will smoke her out. I thought the Bow Street Runners were worried about her disappearance; it did not occur to me they would chase her as a criminal.'

'Can we not go to them, tell them everything we have learnt?' asked Claire.

'I am worried that if we do that, we risk drawing attention to ourselves. I do not trust that the Runners are discreet. We have our pictures, we know the name of the gang, and we know two of the points at which the resurrectionists operate.' Mary swallowed. 'We must be careful not to rouse their attention, lest they should start digging graves for *us*.'

'What are our next steps?' Percy asked.

'We must uncover the identity of the occupier of the house on Hosier Lane.'

\*

The congregation's Evensong sweetened the air as they walked past the church towards Hosier Lane. Mary shivered at the sight of the graveyard and uttered a silent prayer to keep the dead safe as they passed by. A watery moon was lazily pushing itself into the darkening sky; it promised to be ripe and full once sure of itself. Surely that would mean no grave-robbing tonight.

They walked together in silence. All were tired and wanted to bring this sorry matter to a conclusion. Mary's mind whirled. There were still more questions than answers. Who was the woman in the park that Claire had seen? Could she have been the missing Annie Bell? That the woman had died at the hands of Jack Cotton was known, but then who had killed Cotton? Thomas Bell was the natural suspect, given that Annie was his sister, and from what Claire had told her, he knew Jack Cotton. And then there was Mrs Knapp — how did she fit in with it all? She had told them herself that it was difficult to keep good staff, and Thomas had said that she'd had a lot of lodgers recently. Why had she been so quick to cast suspicion on Thomas by lying about him being sent to gather up Annie's belongings?

'This is the place.' James stopped outside the house. It loomed over them in the half-light. Mary crept down the steps to the lowest level and put her hand to the windowpane. A few black flecks of paint peeled away; the window was painted on the outside.

'Knock at the door,' she whispered up to her bemused friends.

'And what shall we say if the door is opened?' Percy asked.

'Say you are collecting money for charity, or you are recruiting for your church — you're a poet, Percy. You'll think of something.'

Percy sighed and stepped up to the door, rapping at the gold doorknocker. Mary heard movement from inside, rustling sounds that were obscured by the blackness of the window; she moved to the small space beside the steps so that she could see the front door.

'Good evening,' she heard Percy say. 'We are collecting alms for the poor.'

Mary twisted her head. The man at the door looked dishevelled; his hair and eyebrows were bushy and unkempt.

'I have no money in this house. Good evening to you.'

The man went to close the door, but Percy's shoe on the gap prevented him from doing so.

'I can see that you are a man of means. Will you not reconsider? Christmas is almost upon us, and people are cold and hungry. We can come in and wait if you need help?'

Mary's pulse quickened. There was a steely determination in Percy's voice that made her heart swell with pride.

'I need no help and will not respond to brute tactics.' The man huffed and stepped back, presumably to shut the door; but it was no good, for Percy's foot was still in it. 'I am a respectable man. I do not expect to be hounded in my home by a gang of ruffians.'

Mary stifled a laugh; in their dress coats and cravats, Percy and James looked nothing like ruffians.

'A respectable man should be a charitable man,' Percy continued, his foot still in the door.

'I have told you, I have no money here. Wait a minute.' The man clicked his fingers. 'If I write you a cheque, will that be enough for you to leave me alone?'

'That would be capital.'

The man disappeared back into the house, leaving the door open. Mary could just make out the yellow flocked wallpaper in the hallway, incongruous with the painted windows. Either the man who lived here was eccentric and private, or he had something to hide; Mary was determined to find out which.

'You are very convincing,' Mary said with a smile to Percy, just as the sound of approaching footsteps echoed down the hallway.

'There! There is your cheque. Five pounds. I think you will find that to be very generous. Now will you leave me alone?'

Percy took the cheque and was about to turn away when something unexpected happened; Claire stepped forward into the doorway and punched the man with one clean, swift blow that sent him reeling backwards to the floor.

'Claire! What have you done?' Mary cried.

'I could not stand any more of his pomposity. Come on, let us look around the house while he is out cold.'

She stepped forward, oblivious to the shocked faces that surrounded her.

'Has she killed him?' Mary asked James.

He swallowed loudly. 'Let us hope not.'

'Percy, James, take him up the stairs, find his bedroom and shut him in it. Hopefully when he wakes, he will think of this as nothing more than a sinister dream.'

'Unless he has the proof of bruising.' Claire laughed.

Mary shook her head; what was going on? First Mrs Knapp's character had peeled away, then Percy's, and now Claire's; thank goodness James was surveying the scene with the same amount of bemused horror as she was.

Percy put the cheque in his pocket, grabbed the man under the shoulders and gestured for James to pick up his legs. They grunted as they heaved the unconscious body up the stairs.

Mary stared at Claire. 'You have knocked the man out so we can look in his house, so where would you have us search?'

'Anywhere, everywhere, but quickly — he will wake up soon.'

Mary moved to the front room, Claire to the one opposite. Mary looked around the darkly decorated room and froze. In place of figurines and ornaments were jars containing ears, eyes and fingers. She gulped at the sight of a solitary eyeball floating in liquid. The nausea that had haunted the early days of her pregnancy returned with a vengeance and Mary swallowed down the bile that rose in her throat. There was a large desk on which papers, quills and inkpots were strewn — not so dissimilar to Percy's working methods. Mary rifled through them, but with no idea of what she was looking for, the task seemed pointless. She paused when she found what appeared to be a clumsily drawn table. At the top were sketches of the moon and numbers beneath them; they seemed to be dates for the different moon phases.

Mary picked it up and put it in her pocket, hurried by the sudden racket of Percy and James's feet stomping down the stairs.

'He is waking up. Let's get out of here.'

James gathered Claire and together they swept through the door, pulling it shut just as the man's voice bellowed behind them. They carried on running all the way down the street, past the church and the graveyard until Mary's lungs ached. So much for Sunday being a day of rest.

'I think that's far enough.' Percy gulped the words out.

Mary held on to her stomach, more to calm the baby than herself. 'What was that, Claire? I thought we agreed we were going to stop putting ourselves in danger, and then you punched that man!'

Claire smiled and held out her open palm.

'It was worth it. I stole the key to the cellar door. Now we can go back and revisit his house whenever we like.'

'I can't believe you did that.' Mary stared at Claire. 'Percy had it under control; there was no need to attack anyone.'

Claire shrugged. 'I got the key to the cellar, didn't I?'

'By the time we go back there — *if* we ever go back there — anything he's hiding will be long gone.'

James had left to attend lectures, and the others returned home. The rooms were freezing cold, resentful of their neglect, and Percy was forced to light a fire. While he poked at it, Claire and Mary prepared a meal of turnip, carrots and potatoes. They were all famished and finished the meal quickly. Mary was happy to finally have some food in her stomach. Now that she was no longer hungry and the room had regained some of its former warmth, they retreated to the sofa.

'Claire, can you pass me my notepad, quill, and ink?'

The items were passed; Mary dipped the quill in the ink.

'The house on Hosier Lane must belong to a man of science because of the exhibit jars in his rooms. What is the name on the cheque he gave you, Percy?'

Percy unfolded the cheque. 'Bartholomew Cooper Paxton.'

'Bartholomew Cooper Paxton.' Mary rolled the words around her mouth. They had a familiar taste, though she couldn't quite place it. 'Cooper Paxton … does that name not seem familiar to you, Percy? Have we not read it in an article or journal?'

Percy's brow creased. 'If we have, I do not recall it.'

'I am sure I know it. Anyway, I suppose the question is, do we suppose him to be a part of this gang of resurrectionists? We know that a body was delivered to his house, but why?'

'Perhaps we could find out if he is affiliated with one of the medical schools; there are not so many to make it impossible to find out. That can be a task for the absent Mr Berry.'

'From the look of his house and the objects within it,' Claire piped up, 'I would assume him to be one of those Gothic eccentrics with a taste for the macabre. It would not surprise me at all to discover that he is conducting ghastly experiments in the cellar.' Everyone laughed, but something in Claire's words struck a chord with Mary — was Cooper Paxton's name associated with the craze for scientific reanimation? She scribbled it down.

'Our next step is to find our Mrs Knapp. We need to uncover her role in all of this.'

Percy sighed. 'And where are the corpses from the graveyard being taken? They may be taken by water or by carriage to various ports, but how long does a body take to rot? Surely there must be conditions for a body to be sold and dissected? Even resurrectionists will have standards!' He clicked his fingers. 'That explains the sawdust on the floor of the cobbler's workshop — it matched the sawdust on the floor of the dissecting room.'

'And the crate!' Mary cried. 'That is why they need boys who work in trades — butchers, cobblers, anyone with access to crates and storerooms, and the men who own the businesses, who can be coerced into helping them or turning a blind eye…'

'Or blackmailed into it. The cobbler bears no resemblance to the man we saw opening up his outbuildings, and his assistant is dead,' Claire added.

'That leaves us with a question — was Jack Cotton hung as a criminal, or was he killed by his own gang?' Mary thought hard. 'And if so, why? For killing Annie?'

Percy turned towards Claire. 'You said that Thomas Bell seemed genuinely angry when he saw the likeness of Jack Cotton. He wouldn't have reacted like that if *he'd* killed Annie.'

If Thomas was angry about the murderer's death, then there was no way he himself had killed Annie. But someone, somewhere, knew what had happened to Annie and Mary was determined to find them.

'If Annie *was* murdered and her body taken for dissection, then it proves that Blaze's men aren't just taking the bodies from the graveyards, but are killing people too.' Mary drummed her fingers. 'But how are they choosing their victims? There must be something we are missing.' She reached for a biscuit. 'Let's go over everything we know about Annie Bell.'

Claire nodded. 'We know she was younger than Thomas and both ran away from home — they probably had a father who was generous with his fists. Thomas left first, then Annie followed, finding a job at a grand house at which some dispute occurred. She then found herself at the mercy of Mrs Knapp, for whom she worked for three months as a domestic servant before disappearing.'

'Mrs Knapp told us that Thomas was sent to collect Annie's belongings, but Thomas told Claire that Mrs Knapp was the one who gathered them together and told him that his sister had disappeared.'

Claire nodded. 'That is correct.'

Mary paused. 'Is it possible that the man you saw in the park did not actually kill the woman? That, sensing your presence, he loosened his grip on her and she sank to the ground in a faint?'

Claire looked thoughtful. 'I suppose it is possible, but I did not hang around to find out.'

Mary nodded. 'You were so shocked by what you saw, or what you thought you saw, that you ran home without stopping or looking back. Correct?' Claire nodded. 'And that was your first instinct, wasn't it? When you thought you were in danger, your first instinct was to run back here to safety?'

'Yes.' Claire shrugged. 'It would be anyone's instinct.'

Percy frowned. 'I don't see what you are getting at, Mary.'

'Claire ran back *here* because this is her home and where she feels safe. And where would Annie go if she felt threatened?'

'Home,' Percy replied.

Mary nodded slowly.

Claire gasped. 'And going home for her meant returning to Mrs Knapp! You think she went back to Mrs Knapp's house and was murdered there?'

'Think about it. When we went back to the park, there was no sign of an altercation except for the scarf. Perhaps Cotton had taken off the scarf in some prelude to seduction; the island is well concealed for courting couples. They may have argued about something, and in a fit of temper he put his hands around her neck. Then Claire disturbed the scene and he fled. So maybe Annie did not die there after all. Perhaps she went back to Mrs Knapp and told her everything — a young woman like that would pour her heart out for a pinch of kindness. And then it was Mrs Knapp that killed her.'

'Thomas Bell might have unknowingly moved the body of his own sister?' Percy asked, his face ashen.

Mary nodded. 'Yes, I'm starting to think that he did. I suppose our next step is to locate this Blaze character and the other players in this criminal set.'

'The barmaid at The Mermaid tavern said she hadn't seen him in a while,' said Percy, 'which tells us that he varies his taverns — touring them all until he's run up ample debt in each, I expect.'

Mary hid a small smile. Was Percy talking from personal experience? The money that his grandfather had promised was yet to materialise, and the days were getting colder. Christmas was around the corner and then the new year and the baby's birth would shortly follow; the thought of spending the spring here with a newborn made her stomach churn.

'Percy,' she said, 'as you are the only one who can do it, I need you to scout out some of the local taverns. Try to stay sober; you must be on your guard for anyone named Blaze. There is a full moon tomorrow night, so Blaze and his associates are unlikely to be graverobbing. They will surely find alternative ways to entertain themselves and, if luck is on our side, they may be out drinking.'

'I should be attending a meeting at the Philosophical Society tomorrow, but I will sacrifice it for the good of the case.'

Mary smiled. She knew Percy would be equally happy ensconced in a tavern with a warm beer.

Claire pouted. 'Might I not go with him? I make a very convincing gentleman.'

'No, Claire, you may not. I need you with me. We are going on the hunt for Mrs Knapp.'

# CHAPTER FOURTEEN

Monday morning brought the sort of winter's day that Mary loved. There was a fresh coolness to the air with no damp mist or fog; it felt as though the world was sleeping and everything was slow to rise, especially the sun, which eventually sent a purple streak across the London skyline. Once the day had started, Mary and Claire made their way to Mrs Knapp's house, presuming that she would not be there but hoping to be able to access her lodgings and discover something that would confirm their suspicions. The early hour meant the children were still abed and their quest was not disturbed by curious neighbours opening windows to bark out warnings.

'The curtains are closed,' Claire whispered. 'Perhaps Mrs Knapp has returned.'

'Or perhaps she left them closed to deter burglars. Come on,' said Mary, picking a pin from her hair. 'We shall go round the back of the house.'

The backs of the houses told a similar tale to the front; paint peeled from window frames, shards of glass had been propped up with wooden panels, and the occasional scurrying sound from the pile of rubbish reminded them they weren't the only creatures somewhere they shouldn't be.

'Has Mrs Knapp any lodgers at the moment?' Claire asked.

'No, I don't think so,' Mary replied, scanning the door. Its timber planks looked flimsy, but it was firmly locked and she did not think that Claire was strong enough to barge it open. 'We didn't see anyone on our visits, and do you recall her complaint that people had been unreliable in their comings and goings?'

A sudden wind betrayed an open window on the first floor, the wooden frame banging.

'You're going to have to climb in through the window and open the door to let me in.'

'Me?' Claire cried. 'How am I supposed to get up there and through the window in this skirt?'

Mary glanced down at Claire's voluminous skirt. She had a point.

'Hold on.' Mary spotted an upturned barrel. 'Give me a hand with this.'

They rolled the barrel into position and stepped back. It seemed to be the right height, but they wouldn't know until Claire climbed up onto it.

'Take off your skirt,' Mary ordered. 'I'll give it back to you when you open the door.'

Claire's face fell. 'Take off my skirt? Crawl through a window in my undergarments? What if a Runner is walking this way?'

'Then he will get more than he bargained for. But you will have a much bigger problem if you get stuck in the window, as there will be no way that I can pull you out.'

Claire rolled her eyes 'Fine!' she huffed.

Mary held the skirt as Claire climbed onto the barrel, steadying herself against the wall.

'If I make it out of this without breaking my leg, it will be a miracle.' The barrel wobbled slightly and, as it did, Claire shrieked.

'Hold on to the window,' Mary hissed. 'Lever yourself up with your hands and slide your body through.'

'What do you think you're doing?' a voice yelled. Mary hardly dared to turn around and see who the voice belonged to; whoever it was, it wasn't good.

'I'm talking to you!' A pebble hit Mary on the back. She swung around, her heart in her mouth. She relaxed when she saw that the voice belonged to a young boy with no shoes. He couldn't be more than eight, but his voice was low and hoarse and he sounded older.

'I'm going to tell my ma; she's supposed to be watching the house for intruders.'

Mary folded her arms, joined by Claire, who had jumped back down from the barrel.

'Do we look like intruders?' Claire demanded. 'Well? Do we?'

Mary tried not to smile at the sight of a skirt-less Claire trying to be serious and authoritative.

The boy swallowed. 'Why haven't you got a skirt on?'

'Because…' Claire trailed off.

The boy folded his arms now. 'You were going to break into her house, weren't you? That's why you was up on that barrel, peering in.'

Mary scratched her head. They were being held to ransom by a child. There was nothing for it but to tell the truth, or at least some of it.

'Mrs Knapp is my friend,' she said. 'We have been trying to get hold of her for days, but we've not heard from her and we're worried. We fear she may have come to some harm.'

The boy stared at her, clearly weighing up all that she had said. Then he nodded slowly. 'My ma says she's gone to escape the men from the clink.' He paused. 'You sure you are friends of hers?'

'We are.' Mary held her swollen stomach. 'Haven't you seen us here before? We've been here many times.' It was a slight exaggeration.

The boy shook his head. 'No, but then I wasn't looking for you, was I?'

'My name is Mary, and this is Claire. We wouldn't be introducing ourselves to you if we meant to rob the place, would we?'

The boy's shoulders relaxed. 'No, I don't suppose you would.'

'And what's your name?'

His shoulders tensed up again. 'Now, I'm not about to tell you that, am I? I'm not a fat-wit.'

'Do you know where Mrs Knapp has gone? I am worried about her, that's all. We are not bailiffs or thieves or anything like that — just friends who want to know that she's safe.'

'She's safe all right.' The boy sniffed. 'We've been looking after her dog.'

'Did she give an address? Or say when she'd be back?'

'She was back last night, but left again early this morning. I thought you were her coming back.'

Coming back on a Sunday, leaving again on a Monday — it brought to mind Percy evading the bailiffs and moneylenders. If money was tight, then that might explain Mrs Knapp's involvement with the resurrection gang — if she was indeed involved with them. They still had no proof other than the word of Thomas Bell that she was. Mary felt a tugging sensation at her hand — it was Claire trying to take back her skirt. Mary passed the skirt back; the boy watched with strange fascination as Claire put it back on.

'There!' Claire trilled. 'Do you still think us to be thieves?'

'I've never met a lady burglar, but that does not mean they ain't real.'

'I'll give you a gold coin if you tell us where Mrs Knapp is,' said Claire, reaching into her purse and digging out a coin. Mary wondered how many more she had squirrelled away in there.

'All right then,' the boy said with a nod, 'but lean in and listen carefully, because I'm only going to say it once.'

The coffee house was full of the smoke of satisfied gentlemen relaxing their time away, unencumbered by responsibility or restraint. Percy's order of vegetables, bread and port were placed in front of him and he rubbed his hands together, overjoyed at the unexpected turn the day was taking. The chair on which he sat was plump and comfortable, and his body sank into it as if it were designed for him. The tablecloth and napkin were of such gleaming white that he had to turn his eyes away from the glare, lest it should cause a migraine. He thought of Mary — as he often did whenever he experienced new things without her — and felt a pang of guilt that he could not bring her here to dine. She might have enjoyed the turtle or the venison forbidden to him. Percy resolved to stop at the market on the way home and secure them something impressive for supper to assuage his guilt.

A long afternoon had been passed going around the taverns and asking if anyone knew of a man called Blaze. Although no one admitted to knowing him, their pale faces and fierce denials confirmed that they knew him by reputation. At the third tavern he had tried, the barmaid had hesitated at the mention of the name. She had told him plainly that Blaze wasn't the sort of man to be messing around with and that he sometimes took his meals at the coffee house across the road. Percy had followed her pointing finger over the street, hoping he had got the right one.

Percy chewed the last of his vegetables and sat back in the chair, his eyelids heavy as he watched the busy London streets beyond the window, people rushing to get home before the heavy darkness swept over the sky like a curtain. He pushed the plate away, picked up the port and sighed. There had been no sign of Blaze, and he did not know how long Mary expected him to wait for a potential lead. He was about to take a long gulp of port when he saw a man scuttle past with an orange scarf tied around his neck. Percy dropped some coins on the table for the meal and hurriedly left the coffee house. The man was in sight but was moving quickly. This called for a canter. Percy — replenished by the food and rejuvenated by the fresh air — was up to the task and soon closed the gap.

The man headed down the passageway behind the shops. Percy followed carefully behind, determined not to lose him. Busy London streets gave way to shadowy neighbourhoods. A full moon this evening might put paid to a bout of graverobbing, but surely that would stop them altogether; where there was money to be made in bodies, surely there were always bodies to be transformed into money. The question was, where would someone find the bodies? Mary and he hadn't discussed the link between the moon almanac discovered at Cooper Paxton's house and the resurrectionist trade or how it would only happen on those nights when the moon did not bear witness to their crimes. Another corner chased another, the route twisting around the shadowy buildings as the night came down. All respectable people had headed home, never touched by these nefarious schemes except as something they saw chronicled in the printed press.

The built-up area fell away and soon Percy was walking through the countryside that paused the hectic city. His heart raced. He did not know where he was going, but it was miles from anything he recognised and there was no way of letting Mary know where he had gone. If he came to another tavern, he could ask about their location and enquire about horses or messengers to get a message to Nelson Square. Percy stopped as a trio of children interrupted his path. This small diversion cost him the sight of the man. He huffed; the man in the orange necktie could be anywhere — how would he ever find him? An arm tightened around his neck. Percy clutched at it, struggling to breathe.

'Why are you following me?'

Percy gasped for air. 'I'm ... not,' he choked.

'That's funny,' said the voice, and a waft of stale ale filled Percy's nose. 'You've been keeping an awful close pace behind me. If you're not following me, then where are you going?'

'I'm going to find Blaze. I've something for him.'

'Something for Blaze? I'll warrant it isn't something he'll want, unless he can sell it.' The arm fell away and Percy coughed, his body collapsing forward.

'Go on then — what is it you have for Blaze?'

'A body.' Percy swallowed frantically.

'A body?' The man moved around until he was face to face with Percy. 'Now, why would a gentleman like you have a body, and what makes you think Blaze would want it?'

'His name was given to me.'

'By who?' The man raised his eyebrows.

Percy trembled but said nothing. There was a brief silence while the man reached into an unseen pocket; then the blade of a knife was cool against Percy's cheek.

'I said, who gave you his name?'

'I overheard it at The Mermaid tavern.'

The blade retreated into its hiding place.

'Seeing as how you're going where I'm going, we may as well take a walk together, like old friends.'

*Old friends don't twist your arm and push it up your back as they march you forward*, Percy thought as he stumbled on; but it was better than a knife to the face, so he let the thought pass. His tried not to twist his ankles as was pushed along like a sack of potatoes; it was quieter here, with less chance of disturbance or help. If he survived this, he would need to purchase some new shoes — it was just as well he had paid his cobbler with his last slice of financial assistance and had given himself more credit. Life was little more than a series of building up and knocking down debts and avoiding people at every turn. Percy's shoulder burned as they approached a row of houses with children playing outside them. They took one look at the man pushing him along and evaporated into the night. Even if Percy didn't know who this man was, the children certainly did.

He scanned the area, desperate to commit as much of it to memory as he could, should he survive long enough to give his version of the evening's events. Percy surveyed the dark common in front of the houses, the area which until moments earlier had been populated by children at play, and for a brief, delicious moment he imagined Mary and Claire running over the common, their skirts billowing out like windswept sails. How he wished to anchor himself to this vision rather than this hateful reality.

'Let's see if he's here, shall we?'

The man knocked on a door with his free hand. Something in the deliberate timing of it was distantly familiar — like a song. Percy shrugged his shoulders, testing the range of his movement and the severity with which he was being held. The grip on his arm tightened. It was useless; there was no getting away now. He sighed heavily. This could not be the way his life ended, not when he had so much more to achieve. The man knocked again, the same knock. The door opened, just a fraction, but enough for Percy to see a woman on the other side of it.

'What are you doing here, Bill?' the woman asked. 'Who's that?' She nodded towards Percy.

'A gift for Blaze. Is he here?'

'What have you brought *him* here for?'

'He says he has a body for us.'

'A body? Whose body?' The woman clutched at her chest. 'You know who this is, don't you? This gentleman is Percy Shelley.' She suddenly gasped. 'Is she here? Is she with you? Oh Lord, don't tell me the body is hers.' She drew a sign of the cross over her chest.

'Do you know what she's talking about?' the man asked Percy, pushing him forward into the house.

Percy held out his hand to keep himself from falling. 'I have never met this woman before,' he replied truthfully.

'We may never have met, but I know all about you,' the woman replied bluntly. 'And I want to know the real reason you are here.'

Mary gasped and retreated back into the shadows.

She and Claire had made their way to St Giles and the address given to them by the boy at Mrs Knapp's house. They had arrived as day turned to night, just in time to witness Percy being manhandled into a dwelling by a brute of a man.

'Why is Percy here? And why has that man pushed him into the house?' Mary's heart quickened and the baby twisted uncomfortably inside her. 'Claire?' She turned to her sister in panic. 'What do we do?'

When she spoke, Claire's voice was firm and decisive, and Mary was grateful for it. 'You stay here, Mary, and make sure they do not leave the house. Create a diversion if you can. I will go and find James and Thomas Bell and bring them here.'

'But they are in the south of the city, and we have traversed all the way to the north; it will be daylight by the time you get there.'

'There is a horse over there, in that field. I will commandeer it.'

'You're going to steal a horse?' Mary's face fell. 'Have you ever ridden a horse before?'

Claire shrugged. 'If Percy can ride a horse, then I'm sure I can too. I will simply follow the route we have taken to get here.'

'But it is dark, and the air has dipped…'

'And the more time we spend talking about it, the greater Percy's danger. You create a distraction here; I'll be back as soon as I can.'

Mary opened her mouth to argue, but Claire was already running across the fields as if propelled by a hurricane. Mary turned back to the house. A figure stood in front of the window. It was Mrs Knapp, her features illuminated by a freshly lit lamp. She leant forward to draw the curtains and, just like that, Mary's view into the room was extinguished.

'What can I do?' she mumbled to herself. 'How do I create a disturbance?'

Mary looked up at the house as she racked her brain for options: she could knock on the door and run back to her hiding place, but that would only give the briefest of intervals. She could go around to the back of the house and see if there was some way of getting in, but with her swollen stomach there was no way she'd be able to climb through a window without getting trapped in it. She could pretend to be a charity collector — as they had at Cooper Paxton's — or a neighbour singing carols of Christmas cheer, but that would only work if there were other houses around, and this one was quite isolated.

'That's it!' she muttered suddenly. She scrabbled on the ground until she found a small rock. Mary picked it up and rolled it in her hands; it was cool and smooth. She squeezed it in her palm, took a couple of steps forward, and then launched the rock towards the window, preparing to quickly retreat at the sound of the shattering glass. When it didn't come, she frowned. Her aim had been way off. Mary sighed, picked up another rock and stepped closer.

This time she didn't miss, and the sound of breaking glass shattered the silence. She ran back to her previous vantage point and watched the house. The curtains were quickly snatched back and Mrs Knapp's face appeared at the broken window.

'Must have been kids,' Mary heard Mrs Knapp say. Mary allowed herself to relax and shifted into a more comfortable position, but instantly regretted it when she heard 'Ha!' from the window. 'There's someone out there, Blaze. Look, over there, behind that hillock.'

Mary froze. There were two shadows in the window now.

'Put him in the trunk, Eleanor. We'll finish him later.'

The male voice carried through the open window, piercing Mary's heart. *Finish him*; that could only mean one thing. They were going to kill Percy, if they hadn't already. She turned and fled, clutching her stomach and skirts as she ran. The night sky had obscured the route and she ran with a blind recklessness.

She didn't have to look back to know that the two figures were behind her, and they were catching up quickly. Mary hesitated, looking around; there was nothing but fields and trees. There was a shed, or some sort of outbuilding, but it was doubtful that she could make it before they caught her. Her heart in her mouth, Mary ran with a renewed sense of purpose: she wasn't just running for her life, she was running for all of their lives.

The cold air made the reins slippery between her fingers, but Claire was determined that she would not fail. The horse had moved swiftly through the countryside, its hooves cutting through the landscape until the quiet fields once more gave way to the busy streets. Claire prayed that James Berry would still be at the hospital; if he was there, then perhaps it would not matter if she found Thomas Bell or not.

She was in luck, arriving just as a host of students were pouring out of the lecture hall and onto the streets.

'James! James Berry!' she shouted into the crowd.

The men all turned and stared at her. It was only to be expected; the sight of a woman desperately trying to stay upright on a horse when her skirts and natural sensibilities had other ideas was sure to attract attention.

James appeared from the crowd. 'Claire?' His voice was laced with doubt. 'Is that you up there?'

'It is, and you need to come with me now!'

Without asking why, he climbed up onto the horse, sitting at the front. Claire gratefully slid backwards, putting her arms around his waist. His body stiffened.

'Don't put your hands there. Wrap them fully around.'

'Of course,' Claire apologised. 'We are going to St Giles. We've found Blaze, and he's got Percy.'

'The resurrectionist?'

'I'll explain on the way. Come on.' She tapped her feet against the side of the horse and the animal bolted forward.

*

'Are you sure there was someone here?' Blaze barked. 'There's no one I can see — probably just kids.'

'I don't know, Blaze.' Mrs Knapp sniffed. 'I could have sworn I saw someone out here, and knowing who is in the house, I think I can guess who it is. Thought she'd have more sense, though.'

'I'm not standing out here all night catching me death, not when I've a body to move and a window to fix. Here, you take the lamp. I'm going back in to find Bill.'

The sound of heavy footsteps grass told Mary that Blaze was retreating to the house. Only Mrs Knapp remained.

'I know you are out here, Mary Godwin.' Mrs Knapp sounded like she was scolding a child playing hide and seek. 'You may as well come out.'

The baby rolled and kicked, making Mary wince. The lamp followed the sound, its shadows dancing on the surrounding walls.

'It's no good, Mary, I know you're here.' Mrs Knapp's footsteps came closer.

Mary held her breath and closed her eyes. Let Mrs Knapp come to her. There was no way she was going to make it easy for her. There was a bucket just out of reach. If she just moved a fraction, she could reach it and use it as some kind of defensive weapon, but that would betray her position. Too late, though her mind had reasoned itself out of it, her hand had sprung out to grab it. Mrs Knapp grabbed Mary's hand and pulled her out from her hiding place.

'Mrs Knapp, stop!' Mary begged, but the old woman's face was contorted into an expression of unfamiliar cruelty — one that Mary supposed may have always been there, lurking under the surface of the practised kindness.

'When Jack described the woman he had seen in Richmond Park, I thought it was you.' Mrs Knapp let go of Mary's arm, replacing it with a firm grip around her neck. 'That was why I sent you that invitation. I'd meant to poison your tea, but when I saw you were pregnant … well, I may be many things, but I'm not a child-killer.'

'You were going to kill me?'

'Yes, I was, and I got a black eye too for my trouble when Jack found out I hadn't done it. I had to pretend you'd run away.'

'You like to pretend that people run away.' Mary spat the words, despite the pressure around her throat. 'Just how many people have disappeared from your lodgings?'

'Enough.' Mrs Knapp pushed Mary down onto the ground. She landed heavily, the air leaving her lungs. 'Getting that rotten house was the only bit of good luck I've had in my whole life, but running houses is an expensive business. Hard enough to pay the bills, let alone put food on the table — the way you were gorging on my biscuits, I think you know all too well about that.'

Mary's cheeks burned as nausea swept over her.

'I'd thought you'd have more sense than to get yourself pregnant by a poet — and a married one at that! Quite the social pariah, aren't you, Mary?' Mrs Knapp's mouth was a cruel, straight line. 'It's going to be hard to shift your bodies. Might have to send them up to Edinburgh — a roaring trade in resurrection up there.'

'Is that where Annie went? Edinburgh?'

Mrs Knapp shrugged. 'As long as he didn't mess her up too much. They want clean bodies up there.'

Bile rose in Mary's throat. Poor Annie. Her first instinct had been correct; it was murder. There was to be no happy ending in this case, no finding Annie safe and well. It had all played out as Claire had seen and as Mary had feared; Annie had been strangled in Richmond Park and then most likely put in a crate and taken all the way to Edinburgh by carriage.

'And Thomas?' Mary stammered. 'Does he know what happened to his sister?'

'He knows her killer is dead and that should be enough for him, unless he wishes to find himself in the same boat. There's no resurrection for a resurrectionist.' Mrs Knapp laughed again.

Mary frowned. Something wasn't quite right. 'If Annie worked for you, why was she murdered? Wouldn't Jack Cotton — knowing her involvement with you and your involvement with Blaze — have been too terrified of retribution to kill her?'

Mrs Knapp shrugged. 'Accidents happen. She shouldn't have got on the wrong side of Blaze. He was always good to her, but she had a wandering eye.'

'Are you saying that Cotton didn't mean to kill her?' Mary paused. The last piece of the puzzle slotted into place. 'He was giving her a warning, wasn't he? A warning from Blaze not to mess around with other men.'

Mrs Knapp didn't respond, so Mary continued. 'But you knew that she'd been seeing someone, and you knew that she had grown close to Blaze. You thought that if they became a couple, he'd have no use for you and you'd find yourself in the crate. Is that somewhere closer to the mark?'

Mrs Knapp laughed. 'What do you know of life? Of love? Caught out by the first man to lay a hand on you! Tell me, Mary, who's the fool here?'

Mary lunged for the bucket, but she hadn't noticed the scythe in the opposite corner; Mrs Knapp ran for it, picking it up at the same time.

'Blaze doesn't know that Annie Bell is dead, does he?' Mary spoke slowly, holding the bucket out in front of her like a shield. 'He doesn't know that you and Cotton were in it together, that you got Thomas Bell to cart his own sister's body away in a crate.'

The scythe was shaking in Mrs Knapp's hands. The grim, pinched expression on her face confirmed all of Mary's suspicions.

'Where did they take Annie's body?' Mary asked. 'They couldn't have taken it to the hospital — someone might have recognised her.' She gasped, the answer obvious. 'They took the crate to Hosier Lane, to Bartholomew Cooper Paxton. Jack Cotton took charge, so Blaze knew nothing about it.'

'What a bag of moonshine!' Mrs Knapp scoffed. 'You haven't got a snuff of proof for any of this.'

'Maybe not.' Mary shrugged. 'But at least I know what happened to Annie, and Thomas Bell will know too.'

Mrs Knapp stretched out the scythe. 'Bell will believe whatever he's paid to believe; they all do. As long as there is ale and money for it, they don't care about the rest.'

'That may be true when it comes to strangers, but not his own sister.'

'Annie Bell was just another stupid girl with an eye for jewels and an ear for flattery; she wasn't special to Blaze. None of them are. I'm the only one he needs.' Her eyes flashed, but her voice shook.

'What happened to Cotton? Did you dispose of him in the same way you killed Annie?' The two women were circling each other now, prowling around like a pair of tigers.

'If you know so much about it all, you tell me.'

'Fine.' Mary swallowed. 'You intended to kill me with poison, but you didn't because I was pregnant; that's how you killed Annie, but it isn't how you killed Cotton.'

'Call yourself a detective? My dog could have deduced that.' Mrs Knapp laughed scornfully. 'Go on, do better.'

'There were no marks on Cotton's neck when I saw his body on the dissection table, no sign of a struggle, and he'd been dead for no longer than a day. The moon was bright that week, so that ruled out any graverobbing; so what else do grave robbers do?' Mary paused. 'They drink. They drink a lot. I think you found him in a tavern, gave him drink until he could hardly stand, persuaded him to come home with you, and while he was passed out, you snuffed the life out of him.'

'Is that so?' Mrs Knapp curled her lip. 'I'm thinking I was too hasty in not getting rid of you.'

Mrs Knapp kicked out at the bucket and it fell from Mary's hands. Mary dived to pick it back up, but Mrs Knapp was quicker, pushing her to the ground, grabbing a handful of her hair and yanking her head back.

'You always were a nosy little thing,' Mrs Knapp snarled. 'You need to learn to keep your mouth shut. So what if I killed Annie Bell and that useless lump of a man? The world's no different a place for having them in or out of it.'

Mary's cheek was slammed against the ground. A sharp, pulling sensation at her stomach made her gasp.

'Wonder if I'll get double the money for a baby,' Mrs Knapp crowed. Pain soared through Mary's body. The heaviness in the pit of her stomach dropped and Mary held onto it, closed her eyes and prayed.

Her eyes were closed too firmly to see the handle of the scythe make impact with Mrs Knapp's head, but the sickening crack, swiftly followed by Mrs Knapp's surprised scream, forced her to look. Thomas Bell was silhouetted in the moonlight, scythe in hand. He stared at it before throwing it to the ground.

'Thomas!' Mary mouthed, her heart pounding — she was still unsure if he were friend or foe. 'How did you know I was here?'

'I didn't.' He shook his head. 'I was going to see Blaze, and I heard voices.'

'How much did you hear?'

'Enough to know she killed Annie.' He sighed wearily. 'And all because she thought she was in with Blaze.'

Mary sat up, struggling to catch her breath. 'And wasn't she?'

'Not in the way she thought.' Thomas shook his head.

'He's got Percy.' Mary trembled as she spoke.

'Who has?' Thomas asked as he helped Mary to her feet.

'Blaze.'

'Blaze has got him?' Thomas sighed. 'Then I'm sorry, Mary, but he's a dead man.'

# CHAPTER FIFTEEN

'He can't be dead. He can't be. I'd know if he was.' Mary shook her head as tears pricked her eyes.

'If there's a chance of making money on a body, Blaze'll take it, no matter who it is.'

'But Percy's a gentleman. He's got a title. He isn't a murderer or a criminal — he doesn't even eat meat. The anatomists will know there's been a mistake.' Mary's voice was hoarse with justifications, but she knew it was no good.

'Blaze won't give two figs about any of that.' Thomas shrugged. 'You get more money for a dead man than a live one. Come on.'

Mrs Knapp lay on the floor, concussed but still breathing. It was only a matter of time until she came round and raised the alarm. A part of Mary wanted to help her, but Thomas grabbed her arm and pulled her away. 'If Blaze has got a body, he'll want it out of his house quickly.'

The house was shrouded in darkness, with only a small circle of light from the gap where someone had tried to patch up the broken window. The front door opened and Mary and Thomas ducked back behind a wall. Mary looked at Thomas; the flash of his orange necktie confirmed he wasn't here because Claire had found him. He was here to work. She still didn't trust that he was on her side, but as he'd saved her from Mrs Knapp, she'd have to take the chance that he was.

'Blaze is expecting you, correct?' she whispered in the dark.

'Yes, what of it?'

'Then you should go and see what's happening. Tell me where you think they'll take Percy, and I'll meet you there.'

'We'll drop the body off at Southwark. Blaze has got no end of men with carriages at his disposal.'

'Where in Southwark?'

'One of his surgeons. Cooper Paxton on Hosier Lane, got that? He won't risk giving a hospital the body of a gentleman.'

'His surgeons?' Mary gasped. 'Is there no end to his network?' There was no way she was telling Thomas that they'd already been to Hosier Lane. He might have helped her against Mrs Knapp, but that was no guarantee that he would help her take on Blaze. Bringing down Blaze would place the noose around his own neck.

Thomas shrugged. 'Like I said, big business in bodies — greater demand than supply, see? Quick, they're coming out.'

'Go, go! Alert the Bow Street Runners if you can! I'll hide here.'

Mary watched the two men carry a crate down the steps.

A tall man with a gentlemanly gait was waving at Thomas. He held a lamp that illuminated the fact that his clothes and bearing had nothing in common with Thomas or the other man she'd watched strong-arm Percy into the house.

Thomas jogged over the ground before disappearing into the gloom. Dizziness overwhelmed her; to think that Percy was in that crate and not knowing if he was dead or alive was almost too much. As Thomas picked up one end of the crate, his head turned — just a fraction — in her direction and she ducked further down, hoping that no one else had seen her. Her hand swept automatically to her stomach; since the earlier burning sensation, there had been no movement there. Mary was suddenly beset by a tremendous fear that she was about to lose everything that mattered to her.

Mary watched the carriage pull away. No sooner had it vanished into the darkness than Claire and James rode onto the scene; the relief was immediate.

'Percy's in that crate!' Mary cried, pointing after the carriage. 'They are headed to Hosier Lane.'

'We can catch it,' said James. Claire reached down to help Mary up onto the horse. Once in place, she clung to Claire's waist.

James pulled at the reins and the horse made a sharp turn. Mary held on tightly to Claire. The turn negotiated, Mary was impressed by James's deft handling of the horse and knowledge of the dark landscape of London. Nothing was too difficult or unexpected, and the horse's speed seemed to show its confidence in James's navigation skills. Moving back through the swollen heart of industrial London, the horse kept an even line regardless of the shops, taverns, and houses that sought to attract the eye.

There was no sign of the carriage and fear flamed up inside her; perhaps it had been a trick, a way of throwing her off the scent? Tears welled in her eyes and were promptly dashed away by the night air.

'There's a carriage over there.' James pointed towards a distant speck on the horizon. 'Yes, it's definitely going to Hosier Lane. It has just missed the turn for the cemetery. Come on – we can get there before it.' James pulled at the reins and kicked his heels into the sides of the horse, who recognised the command to go and instantly regained its former speed.

The horse galloped through the streets. Mary's knuckles were as white as her face; she gulped as the horse made its way through the landscape, surrendered now to row upon row of houses pushed together like boxes. Then James pulled on the reins and brought the horse to a stop outside a tavern. He jumped down and tied the reins to a lamp post.

'Did Percy ask you if you had heard of Bartholomew Cooper Paxton?' Claire asked.

'Heard of him? Who hasn't? He is the most eminent surgeon in the land,' James replied. 'I cannot believe he has a part in this.'

'We believe he has the body of Annie Bell.' Mary paused. '*Had* the body of Annie Bell.'

She thought back to the evening that had started it all; if only she hadn't written such scornful remarks in her journal, Percy would never have gone to sail his burning boat and Claire would not have been witness to the violence which had resulted in Annie's murder. But it wasn't just about one murder now; who knew how many lives had been snuffed out, how many bodies had been laid out on dissecting tables throughout the land for unsuspecting students with no idea of the depravity that had brought them there? Mary shuddered; she could not allow herself to think of Percy as one of them.

James held out a hand to help Mary down from the horse. Claire had already jumped off with one magnificent sweep of her leg, but it wasn't so easy for Mary. She clutched her stomach with one hand, moved her legs over the side and allowed herself to slide into James's arms. She hovered there for a moment as something flickered between them before she shook the thought away.

'Quickly,' James whispered. 'I can hear the carriage approaching.'

They made their way to the house, grateful for the broken lamp that masked their movements. Claire pulled out the key that would let them into the cellar and fumbled with the lock.

Once inside, muffled voices and laughter travelled down through the floorboards. It was as dark as the street and they navigated the space with outstretched arms.

Two odours fought for prominence in the air: a turgid, artificial smell that grabbed the throat — a similar smell to one at the Royal College of Surgeons — and another that reminded Mary of the time she had found a dying bird and had unsuccessfully attempted to nurse it back to life. It was a damp, earthy smell. Neither were pleasant.

'What is that chemical smell?' Mary whispered.

'Potassium chlorate,' James answered.

Underneath all was the smell of wood. Mary crouched down and felt the sawdust beneath her shoes. It linked the cobbler's workshop, the Royal College of Surgeons and Cooper Paxton's house together; all had seen the same foul deeds and wore their odours.

'Are there any lamps?' Mary's hands fell upon a smooth surface she took to be a table or workbench.

'Here.' James struck a match. The flame danced between his fingers. It illuminated the dark space long enough for Mary to see that she'd placed her hand on a dissecting table and that the decomposing body on it belonged to a young woman. Rearing back, she caught a glass bottle and sent it crashing to the floor. The voices from above stopped and were replaced by the sound of hurried footsteps.

'Quick, we have to hide,' Claire whispered.

Mary pointed to the black cloth that skirted the table and they darted underneath it, James blowing out the flame.

'You left the cellar door open,' came Cooper Paxton's voice.

'No, I didn't. I never leave the door open, except for deliveries.'

'Are you expecting one this evening?'

'No.'

Mary held her breath. Now she could hear the horses' hooves as the carriage creaked to a stop outside.

'Well, whether or not you are expecting one, there's a carriage here. It's Blaze.'

A draught from the open cellar door blew at the skirt of the table.

The footsteps went outside, and the door was firmly shut behind them.

'What are we going to do?' Claire whispered.

'Come on.' Mary crawled out from underneath the table and ushered Claire and James to follow her. Together they crept up the stairs, which revealed a door with a latch at the top. Mary pushed it open with a muffled creak, permitting them to enter the main house while its occupants were preoccupied with the carriage. Mary stopped and stared down the hallway to the front of the house as the men manoeuvred the crate into their arms. She recognised two of the men with Cooper Paxton as the surgeons who had delivered the demonstration at the Royal College of Surgeons — Dr Harper and Dr Hume. She glanced at James, who was staring at them in wide-eyed disbelief.

'Did you know they were in on it?' she whispered.

'I did not,' James replied coolly. 'Are there no honest men left in London?'

Mary did not have an answer for that question so didn't reply. Instead they watched from the shadows at the back of the house as an argument unfolded at the front. Cooper Paxton was gesturing for the men to bring the crate in and as they did so, Mary glimpsed Thomas Bell; his expression was pure thunder.

The front door slammed, and the action moved to a room at the front of the house. Mary, Claire and James crept closer, their footsteps masked by the increasing volume of the voices. Something was happening, something that had taken the group by surprise. There were furious sounds of slaps and punches, followed by bodies slamming against wooden surfaces and the floor. Mary peered round the doorway. Bill's body lay on the floor, Thomas Bell in front of it, his hands curled into bloodied fists. Mary quickly scanned the rest of the room; the crate was still closed, and the surgeons and Blaze had taken up position behind it. Claire and James had fallen in behind her.

'Berry, thank goodness you are here! This man has broken into our meeting and is threatening our lives,' said one of the surgeons — Dr Hume, Mary thought.

Before James could react, Thomas spoke, his gaze fixed on Blaze. 'I know all about your relationship with Annie and how Mrs Knapp killed her. Is she here?'

Blaze sniffed. 'Annie left. I know nothing else about it.'

Mary watched Thomas march forward, his eyes wild with rage. He stopped by the crate and with a huge roar kicked out at it, breaking the lid loose. Mary gulped, her heart fluttering in her chest, a weak flame. Then Percy burst out, gulping air greedily, like a man half-drowned.

'Percy!' Mary rushed towards him, knocking them both down with the weight of her relief and affection. She kissed him without a care, her cheeks wet with tears. The baby stretched out comfortably in her stomach; the equilibrium of her world restored.

'Of all the depths you'd sink to, I never thought you'd kill off one who'd done so much to help you and nothing to hurt you.' Thomas shook his head at Blaze. 'Annie and Jack Cotton meant nothing to you, did they?' He reached into his pocket and withdrew a pistol. 'I want to see my sister.'

Claire stepped forward. 'Thomas, it's too late for Annie, but it's not too late for you. Take all the money you can get from them, get out of London, and start a new life.'

'What about you, Claire? Will you come with me?'

'If you want, yes.'

Mary bit her lip. What was Claire playing at? Surely, she couldn't seriously be contemplating a life with Thomas Bell?

'Thomas, Annie is here,' Claire continued, her voice soft, her hand gently resting on his arm. 'But please don't see her. It will do you no good — remember her instead with life and vitality.' She hesitated. 'Remember her with love.'

'That's a lovely sentiment, Claire.' Thomas patted her hand with his. 'But I need to see her for myself. Where is she?'

'She's downstairs, in the cellar.'

Thomas waved the pistol at Blaze, Cooper Paxton and the two surgeons. 'Lead the way,' he snarled. 'Any funny business and I'll shoot.'

'Can you walk?' Mary whispered to Percy. He nodded, and they followed with James and Claire.

'I need a lamp.' Thomas's demand was soon met, and Claire held the lamp, which quivered in the air; Mary knew her sister was afraid, but was helpless to do anything about it.

'When he is distracted by the body, I will grab for the gun,' James whispered to Mary and Percy. 'Be ready.'

There was no time to argue as they traipsed down the stairs to the cellar. Thomas was standing in front of the body of his sister, or what was left of it. The lamp revealed the grisly extent of the scene, a carved chest revealing spaces where organs had been extracted. Only the long blonde tresses hinted at the woman Claire had seen in the shadows of Richmond Park. She turned away, her face pale. Thomas stared at the corpse, his expression unreadable. Mary wondered if he were looking at the consequences of his crimes for the first time.

'I never really thought about what happened afterwards.' Thomas's voice was flat, all traces of emotion extinguished. Mary's skin prickled; this was when a man was at his most dangerous. 'I thought only about the money. I never stopped to think that these were people with lives and family who loved them.' He turned steely eyes on Blaze. 'Robbing graves is one thing — those people ain't coming back — but to take a life like this, to rob our Annie of a future, all because she had the bad luck to meet Mrs Knapp… I can't forgive that.' The gun was pointed at Blaze. 'I hope you believe in the Devil, Blaze, because you are about to meet him.'

'Thomas, no!' Claire cried out.

The gun went off; two loud shots rang through the air. Mary turned just in time to see James launch himself towards Thomas as the gun fired again. He knocked Thomas to the ground and the gun fell to his feet. Claire rushed to grab it, pointing it towards the criminals, the weapon unsteady in her shaking hands. Thomas reached for the gun, but was knocked to the ground by a punch from Percy. Calmness returned to the scene like a slowly released breath.

'He's been shot!' Mary gasped. Blood seeped through James's white shirt, blossoming into a violent rose on his chest. 'Fetch a surgeon, quickly!'

James clutched at his chest, shaking his head. 'If I die having rid the world of a gang of resurrectionists, I will consider it a fair legacy.'

'But I will not!' cried Mary. 'Percy, Claire, hold him up. Let's take him upstairs.'

The Bow Street Runners had arrived during the chaos and had control of the scene below; their firm hold on Thomas

Bell and Blaze reassured Mary that they weren't going anywhere. They would not add another murder to the night's tally.

'Bring your medical bag!' Mary shouted back to Paxton Cooper, who shifted uneasily, anxious as a deer.

James shook his head. 'No, I will not be seen to by him. It is a flesh wound; I can direct Mary and Claire to see to it. All we need are the surgical instruments.'

'Can we?' Claire asked. 'I'm not sure I feel confident in this.'

'I will give direction,' Berry said weakly. 'But only you two, otherwise I choose to die.'

'We will not let that happen,' said Mary firmly, shaking her head. 'Percy, get the bag and stay with the Runners.'

Percy took the bag from the surgeon and ushered them into the front room, closing the door behind him as he left.

'Mary, Claire, you are the only people I trust with this, but you must promise to keep my secret,' James stammered.

Mary nodded and opened the bag. All the implements looked torturous and her hands shook at the sight of them. 'What am I looking for? What are we to do?'

'The bullet must be extracted and the skin sewn up.' James winced as he spoke. 'Claire, fetch salted water from the kitchen for the wound while I instruct Mary on how to extract it.'

Claire nodded and left the room. James turned his head to watch her go and indicated his shirt.

'Mary, you must unbutton my shirt.'

Mary bit her lip, peeled the jacket away from the shirt, untucked it at the source, and tried not to panic at the sight of all the blood that stained the shirt. Her fingers trembled as she fumbled with the buttons. 'What next?'

'Now you must lift the shirt and take off the bandages.'

'Bandages?' Mary frowned. 'Are you already injured?'

James smiled weakly before grimacing. 'Only by society, Mary, only by society.'

Adrenaline spiked through her body, and she worked diligently, keen to keep to the letter of James's instructions. The bandages were located and she found a pocketknife in the bag.

'Will this do to cut the bandages?'

'If you use a flame on the knife, it will also do to cut out the bullet.'

Mary nodded again, willing her mind to full concentration; the bandages were flush to the skin and there was scarcely any space for her to slide the knife underneath. James wriggled beneath her, his hand clutching the site of the wound. She needed to be quick and accurate. She gulped as the blade bit through the fabric, loosening it strand by strand until it fell back, revealing the curves of a breast.

'I don't understand,' Mary whispered.

'I'm a woman, Mary,' James replied. 'Now, hurry and take this bullet out before Claire returns.'

A million questions flooded Mary's mind, but she had a job to do and focused instead on that. She gritted her teeth, waved the flame through the open neck of the oil lamp, then took the head of the knife to the circle of the wound. James grimaced.

'Sorry, sorry,' Mary apologised, gently nudging the knife in until she felt the end of the bullet. 'I've got it!' she cried.

'Push it out quickly, then sew it up.'

The door opened. Claire saw the exposed torso and gasped, nearly dropping the bowl of water. She hurriedly shut the door and knelt beside Mary.

'No need to look so shocked, Claire,' Mary said. 'It isn't as if you don't have a pair of your own. Now, give me the saltwater, and find me something to stitch James up with.'

Claire passed it over wordlessly, her mouth gaping open and closed like a confused fish. Mary tended to the wound with the saltwater, which made James grimace once again. Then she threaded the needle, running it through the flame before bringing it to the skin.

'Are you sure you wouldn't prefer this to be completed by a qualified surgeon?' Mary's hands trembled so much she could hardly hold the needle.

'And be thrown out of a medical career because of my gender? No thank you!'

Claire spoke at last. 'Give it to me, Mary. I was always much better at needlecraft than you.'

Claire took to the sewing with a steadiness Mary did not possess. Mary held her shaking, clammy hands together.

'Presumably you aren't really called James Berry?' Claire asked as she stitched up the wound with neat crosses.

'Of course I am called James Berry.'

'But you weren't born James Berry.'

'No, but I shall live and die as him. Is that not enough for you?'

'That is as much as anyone needs to know.' Mary chided, tutting at Claire. 'What an exciting life you lead!'

'Believe me… Ow, careful!' James hissed. Claire mouthed apologies and carried on stitching. 'I would prefer to qualify as a woman and have a career as a woman, but society will not let women of our class have any career, let alone a medical one.'

'We may be companions, guardians or teachers — hateful professions all.' Claire stopped, shuddered, then resumed her work. 'There.'

'If we rip up the shirt, we may use it as a bandage,' Mary said.

'Or we could check to see if there are any bandages in the bag?' Claire said.

'Oh, yes.' Mary delved into the bag, finding clean, white fabric that would make an ample replacement for the bind.

'One day, may I ask you more about it?' Claire's eyes widened as she and Mary fixed the bandage into position.

'If I survive this, then I will take you out for tea and you can both ask all the questions you like; but you must swear never to tell another living soul.'

'Why would we?' Claire smiled. 'I love keeping secrets.'

For a moment, Mary wondered what secrets Claire might keep, but decided it would be better not to know.

'There, all done.'

The bullet rested on the bloodstained bandage. James's face was restored to its usual hue and Mary couldn't quite believe that they had somehow averted disaster; perhaps they were more resilient than she thought. A knock on the door was followed by Percy's voice.

'Everything well in there? The Runners are taking them all to Bow Street.'

'Ready?' Mary and Claire knelt on the floor on either side of James and helped him up.

'You're looking better, Berry,' said Percy as they opened the door. 'Perhaps we shall make nurses of Mary and Claire yet.'

'We make much better detectives,' Mary said with a wry smile. 'I think we will leave the future of medicine in James's capable hands. Don't you agree, Claire?'

'Definitely.'

# EPILOGUE

## *Christmas Day, 1814*

The Christmas table was heaving with delights. Percy had more parsnips and potatoes than he could eat in a year, and there was meat, mead, and merriment enough for everyone else. William Godwin and Mary Jane were being suspiciously hospitable, and a convivial atmosphere pervaded the air and renewed Mary's spirits. It had been a successful Christmas day, full of good cheer and food and drink enough to see them through to the next one.

'Mary! Mary, wake up!' Claire's voice broke through and as Mary opened her eyes she realised it had all been a distant dream.

'Coming,' Mary yawned. Claire had taken it upon herself to cook the Christmas dinner and Mary marvelled at the table, the goblets glittering in the sun streaking through the window.

'The table looks lovely, Claire. Thank you.'

It looked even more glorious for Percy's face shining from the seat at the top of the table.

'We were wondering if you'd sleep through to Boxing Day!' James laughed, pouring wine into the goblets.

'Just because we saved your life, it doesn't give you the right to be impertinent to us for the rest of it,' Mary replied with a smile. 'Merry Christmas!'

She sighed happily. She'd never felt more content to be alive and more grateful for the people sitting at the table; the absence of any Christmas greeting from her father or stepmother had hurt a little, but the pain of their loss was more than compensated for by the outpouring of love from her friends. Children ran outside the houses, taking to the cold streets to burn off their excess energy or to share songs and greetings with their neighbours. Mary looked outside and smiled; there was a delicate frosting of snow on the ground and the children cheered and whirled around, catching snowflakes in their hands. For a brief moment she thought she saw the ghostly figure of Mrs Knapp standing across the road. Her heart thudded. Would she always be looking over her shoulder, afraid that Mrs Knapp would come for her? Her disappearance from Blaze's house had surprised everyone. No. Mary doubted she would ever be heard from again.

Sighing, she turned back to the joyous scene at the table; Percy had bought her a notebook and quill, which made her laugh merrily when he had opened the same gifts from her. From Claire, she had received a copy of the latest Byron, and the latest Humphry Davy from James. It had been a year of ridiculous highs and lows, but as 1814 drew to a close she totted up all that she had achieved: romance and elopement with Percy, adventures in Paris and London with Claire, the solving of two cases, the reading of countless books and the eating of insufficient numbers of biscuits. She cradled her stomach gently. Next year would bring a whole new chapter of her life, and it was one she could not wait to read.

# A NOTE TO THE READER

Dear Reader,

I hope you have enjoyed your whirlwind adventure with Mary, Percy and Claire trying to locate *The Lost Girls*. This is the second of my Mary Shelley Investigations books with Sapere Books and I am relishing the opportunity to bring Mary Shelley to life. In my first book, *The Missing Wife*, we met Mary and Percy at the start of their relationship. They had eloped to Paris, so everything was fresh and exciting, but in this second book we bring them back to London where the situation is very different.

Mary, Percy and Claire were forced back to London after running out of funds during their travels. Percy, still married to Harriet Westbrook at the time, was seen to have brought shame to his family name, so money and opportunities were limited. Mary's father, William Godwin, refused to acknowledge the union and they found themselves at the centre of a great scandal and completely broke. Reading Mary's journals and letters from this time gives a real sense of the pressures they were facing and the stark difference between the excitement of the elopement and life in a succession of small, rented apartments:

*Monday 24th October*

*Read aloud to Jane – at eleven go out to meet S- Walk up and down Fleet Street – call at Peacocks – return to Fleet Street – call again at Peacocks – return to Pancrass remain an hour or two – People call – I suppose bailiffs – return to Peacocks – call at the coffee house – see S. – he has been to Ballachy's = good hopes -to be decided Thursday morning –*

*return to Peacocks – dine there – get money – return home in a coach – go*
*to bed soon tired to death.*

Certainly, Mary's life in September 1814 was very different to life only three months earlier. By the autumn they were continually playing cat and mouse with a succession of bailiffs, and Percy's presence or absence depended on the time and day of the week (bailiffs could not chase for money on a Sunday, so Percy often returned home then). Mary was heavily dependent on their remaining friends for money and food, and it was a good job she was a keen reader and able to while away the time in relatively inexpensive and solitary pursuits, as social calls and opportunities were few and far between. I loved the idea of Percy Shelley making paper boats and floating them down the lakes and rivers of London. Given that he had a fear of water and was unable to swim, this gentle pursuit speaks volumes about his childlike innocence and love of simple things, though I couldn't help but put a murder in there (sorry, Percy!).

As with the first book, I have sought opportunities to weave this story alongside existing information about the Shelleys' lives. I chose their return to London as it provided a chance to explore themes of science, medicine and resurrectionists. Mrs Knapp was the name of Mr Godwin's landlady at his house with Mary Wollstonecraft at the Polygon, so it seemed a natural choice for the 'kindly' woman Mary knew in her youth. Doctor James Berry is based on Doctor James Barry, who was the UK's first female-born doctor. Barry, who was born Margaret Anne Bulkley in Ireland in 1789, became a military surgeon in the British Army and performed the first successful caesarean section. Despite living in a time of restrictive gender roles and limited opportunities for women, Barry was an early pioneer of LGBTQ+ rights and just the sort of hero Mary Wollstonecraft and Mary Shelley would champion.

The ebbs and flows of life are so attractive to a writer, and from reading Mary Shelley's journals and letters it is interesting to see how the dynamics shifted between Mary and Claire throughout this time period. In their real lives (as documented) there were question marks over the nature of Claire's relationship with Shelley and many indications that Mary believed it had become sexual. Tensions between the two women definitely seemed to come to a head now that Percy and Mary were no longer dependent on her ability to speak French. Mary's pregnancy and Percy's many absences meant that there was a forced friendship between them, a sense of community in their mutual exile; that Claire was jealous of Mary there is no doubt, but Mary also appeared to be jealous of Claire's relationship with Percy at times.

There are also many entries that offer contradictory information about the nature of Shelley's relationship with Harriet after his elopement with Mary, and I have used information from Mary and Percy's journals to inform the sections where Percy is desperate to meet his newborn son Charles. Mary seemed to turn a blind eye to Percy's behaviour on many occasions and in many different ways — the true sign of a woman in love. There are also claims that Mary refused the advances of Thomas Peacock and Thomas Jefferson Hogg, despite Percy's interest in exploring free love as part of his vision for a utopian society.

*The Diary of a Resurrectionist 1811-1812* by Bailey James Blake was a fascinating source of information on the themes of resurrection and medicine, and I used this research to inform the work of Blaze's gang. For me, it is important to trace all the threads that might have contributed to Mary's ideas for

*Frankenstein*, and I like to think that she too would have had a fascination with all the murkier aspects of science and anatomy during this thrilling period. It is true that Percy Shelley fainted during an anatomical demonstration and dissection, but with artistic licence I have changed the time and place of it from his student days at Eton College to his time in London with Mary.

If you enjoyed *The Lost Girls* and would feel comfortable leaving a review on **Amazon** or **Goodreads** that would be greatly appreciated. I hope you have enjoyed your adventure with Mary and Percy and will come back to follow them on their next adventure in London! I'm always delighted to hear from my readers, so if you would like to connect with me follow me at **@donnagowlandwrites** on Instagram and **@DLGowlandWrites** on X.

**Sapere Books** is an exciting new publisher of brilliant fiction and popular history.

To find out more about our latest releases and our monthly bargain books visit our website:
**saperebooks.com**